Recognition Factor

A Denise Cleever
THRILLER

CLAIRE
McNAB

Bella
BOOKS

Ferndale, Michigan
2002

Bella Books, Inc.
P.O. Box 201007
Ferndale, MI 48220

Printed in the United States of America on acid-free paper
First Edition

Editor: Greg Herren
Cover designer: Bonnie Liss (Phoenix Graphics)

ISBN 1-931513-24-4

For Sheila

Acknowledgments

As always, my deep appreciation for the efforts of my eagle-eyed editor, Greg Herren, and my incomparable, anonymous Typesetter.

CHAPTER ONE

"Are you worried about the meeting?"

I gave Cynthia an incredulous look. "Me? You're joking."

I would have died rather than admit I was nervous, although my stomach felt hollow. This meeting was a big deal. The United States had sent representatives to Canberra from the FBI, the CIA, and Homeland Security. On our side, apart from ASIO people, there'd be personnel from the Federal Police and the super-secret Defense Intelligence Organization.

And I, Denise Cleever, was to be the center of attention. Why? Because I was the only Western intelligence agent who had seen the terrorist code-named Red Wolf and lived.

The fact that I alone might identify this elusive international terrorist who'd been tied to key political assassinations, devastating bombings, and the overthrow of certain third-world governments, gave me a certain notoriety in the intelligence community. The consensus at ASIO — the Australian Security Intelligence Organization — was that I probably wouldn't recognize Red Wolf if I ran into him again. After all, I'd hardly seen him under optimum conditions. It had been at night and at the height of a tropical storm.

It was difficult to get comfortable on the polished wooden bench outside Meeting Room 4. I jiggled my feet, smoothed the skirt of my navy suit — I'd been given strict instructions to dress up for the occasion — and glanced at my watch. The hands had hardly moved. Perhaps it needed a new battery.

"Are you all right?" said Cynthia, my ASIO control, eyeing me narrowly. Her spiky hair seemed subdued, and her usually mobile face was tense and unsmiling. And more tellingly, her angular body was clad in an uncharacteristically plain, dark green dress.

I gave her my best confident smile. "Cynthia, I could hardly feel better."

Her lips quirked at my deliberate use of her real name. For security reasons, Cynthia took a different pseudonym for each undercover assignment she directed. In all our briefing sessions together, I used whatever name she'd assigned herself, and she called me by my undercover moniker.

We'd first met after I moved into undercover work and she became my first, and so far only, control. I'd called in from the field to speak to a Livia, Cecily, Myra, Polly, Roderica . . . and each time Cynthia's angular, uncommon self would be at the other end of the line.

Although I'd never admitted it to her, Cynthia's voice had often been a warm comfort to me when I'd been in the field and had felt overwhelmed or apprehensive. Indeed, my qualms about the coming assignment sprang not only from the fact that I'd be in unfamiliar territory, but the knowledge

I wouldn't have Cynthia directing me. Instead, I'd have some American I'd never met.

"About my new control," I said, "have you heard anything yet?"

Clearly exasperated, but also amused, she raised one circumflex eyebrow. "How many times have you asked me? A hundred? You'll probably know before I do."

We both looked up as the door to the meeting room opened. A middle-aged woman I'd never seen before poked her head out. "Five minutes," she said in our general direction. In a perfunctory tone she added, "Sorry to keep you waiting."

After the woman disappeared, I observed, "She wasn't the slightest sorry. In fact, she seemed quite smug. Triumphant, even."

Cynthia looked at me with a hint of impatience. "You're going to be serious in there, I hope."

"Positively somber. Grave, if you like."

She gave me a half smile. "Sedate would be quite sufficient."

"I promise not to make a single joke."

"It's no joking matter." Abruptly, she was serious. "Denise, you don't have to volunteer for this. There's no compulsion and there'd be no recriminations if you backed out, even at this point."

"I'm the only one who'd know him, face to face, aren't I? Or do you think I won't recognize Red Wolf when I see him?"

Cynthia shrugged. "I'm not worried about you recognizing the man. What concerns me is what happens afterwards."

There was no answer to that. It concerned me too. In that one close encounter with the terrorist, I'd been outside in wet darkness, holding on for dear life while I peered into the lighted bridge of the catamaran. When a shout alerted him that there was an intruder on board, had there been enough reflected light for Red Wolf to see my features clearly?

Logic told me no — my fears whispered otherwise.

ASIO analysts had determined that a fleeting glimpse though rain-spattered glass on a vessel heaving in wild seas would only result in a blurred impression of a face. I was about to find out the hard way if they were correct.

I'd actually had two glimpses of the master terrorist. If I shut my eyes I could visualize the first. The little dock had been lashed by wind and rain. Its single light, set on a pole, had been vibrating with the unrelenting force of the breaking waves. Red Wolf was an indistinct figure striding along the wet boards, baseball cap pulled down over his eyes, the wind snatching at his clothing.

He'd struck me then as small and insignificant, although the captain of the waiting catamaran had shrunk back as if menaced. I remember how I'd squinted through the wet darkness to see the terrorist's face without success. The best I could do was estimate his height and build, and commit to memory the way he walked and held his head.

My second view of him through the rain-streaked window of the catamaran's bridge had shown me his face. He'd been almost shocking in his normality. Mr. Average, with nothing notable about him. I'd been so concentrated in mentally recording his facial characteristics that the gun clenched in my hand, the bucking vessel and the tumult of the storm had receded to the edge of my consciousness.

It seemed I'd been debriefed a thousand times since then, but the renditions of Red Wolf's face, created both with computer facial identification programs and from sittings with police artists, had never quite captured the man I'd seen.

So often I'd gone over that one moment when I could have killed him — to save, by pulling a trigger, the lives of so many future victims — but I'd hesitated, and the opportunity was lost. Now it looked like I might have another chance.

The door to the meeting room opened again. "We're ready for you now," said the woman. Disconcertingly, she directed a toothy grin at me. "Come right on in."

"Lamb to the slaughter," I murmured to Cynthia. She didn't smile.

The preliminaries had taken some time. I'd been ushered to a seat at one end of the huge, polished table. Conversation stopped as everyone looked in my direction. It had been uncomfortable to be the focus of such concentrated assessment, so I kept my face expressionless as I took a sip of water from a crystal glass. The woman who'd ushered us into the room appeared with coffee for me. I noticed the coffee cup was not the customary plebian mug, but fine bone china. Obviously no expense was spared at this level of international intelligence meetings. Our tax dollars at work.

Cynthia had gone to the opposite end to sit beside Bernard Byrd, ASIO bigwig. The Director was an overweight, gray man with a fleshy face and a pretentious manner. His pinstriped suit was rumpled and his tie askew. It would be easy for someone who didn't know him to dismiss him as a pompous fool, but I knew he was anything but stupid. Underneath his exterior of infuriating mannerisms lurked a keen mind.

I nodded politely to each person as Byrd went around the table intoning names. There were ten men present, but only three women, excluding me and Cynthia. I'd been briefed on who would be present at the meeting, and I took special notice of Lawrence O'Donnell of Homeland Security. He had a square head set on a thick neck, a thin-lipped mouth and hooded eyes. As one of the American president's confidants, he wielded great influence. An almost palpable aura of power surrounded him. His very presence indicated the importance being placed on this meeting by the Americans.

O'Donnell had a yes-man next to him, a rabbity guy named Flynn, who had not much chin and even less hair. He kept whispering to his boss. O'Donnell jerked his head once or twice in acknowledgement, but otherwise appeared to ignore whatever he was being told.

The majority of the people at the table regarded me with curiosity. I couldn't imagine what they had to be curious about, as each had no doubt read the comprehensive dossier that outlined everything anyone needed to know about my life and career. One of the two FBI agents, a black woman named Leota Woolfe, smiled warmly, but on the whole the atmosphere in the room was solemn.

On my right was an FBI agent from Los Angeles called Maddie Parkes, who had a maddening sniff. Otherwise, she was quite prepossessing, having a neat body, sleek reddish hair and an interesting, slightly asymmetrical face.

"Sinus problems?" I said.

"Allergies." She sniffed again for emphasis. "Martyr to allergies. You?"

"Allergy-free."

"Lucky. I've got severe post-nasal drip."

Several flippant replies tempted me, but aware that Cynthia was watching me with an admonishing air, I contented myself with saying, "Must be a trial."

"You've no idea. And *spring* . . ." Maddie Parkes shook her head. "Fuhgeddaboutit!"

"Well, people . . ." Bernard Byrd hauled himself to his feet, taking off his reading specs as he did so. They remained dangling in one hand, and would, I knew from experience, be used to punctuate his discourse. Silence fell, except for a muffled snuffle from the woman beside me.

"Humph," he began, looking around the table as though mentally marking an attendance list. "Now that we have Agent Cleever present, I believe we can get to the meat, the nub, the gist of the meeting." Bernard Byrd had a sonorous, self-important voice, and I could see a hint of impatience on several faces.

"First, I hardly need remind you all of the necessity of total security regarding the matters before us today. Literally,

6

without a modicum of exaggeration, a matter of life and death." A meaningful pause to let this sink in, was followed by, "Second, I'm keenly aware that each one of us has been exhaustively briefed, but I believe it behooves me to provide a short summation of the exigent circumstances."

I resisted rolling my eyes. Bernard Byrd loved words like *behooves*. It was not for nothing that in ASIO he was called Boring Bernie behind his back. At the last briefing where he'd addressed us on *The New Face of Terrorism*, he'd slipped in so many obscure words that there'd been rolling eyes galore.

No one in this gathering seemed impressed by ASIO's VIP. Several people rustled papers, and Lawrence O'Donnell frowned heavily. Bernard Byrd was not discouraged, gesturing extravagantly with his specs as he said, "All the indications are, as intensive intelligence work on several continents has indicated, that the international terrorist, known to the world in general by the sobriquet Red Wolf — I might mention a suitably lycanthropic appellation for such a miscreant — will be in California, more particularly, Los Angeles, to coordinate some as yet unascertained terrorist operation. This man is not driven by principle, but by greed. At various times he's numbered among his clients Lebanon's Hezbollah, Palestine's Hamas, the Kurdish PKK, the Tamil Tigers, various militia groups, the IRA, even individuals with some psychotic agenda to follow —"

"If I may . . ."

O'Donnell had put up a hand, obviously intending to interrupt the flow, but ASIO's pride ploughed on. "As this terrorist has contrived with skill, not to mention a measure of good fortune, to remain faceless as far as Western intelligence organizations are concerned, it is of great import that" — he broke off to stab his specs in my general direction — "one of our agents has actually seen this man's features, and lived to tell the tale."

"Everyone here is aware of the situation," said O'Donnell. "We've discussed the matter exhaustively, and I see no reason to rehash it yet again." He had a hard voice to go with his hard persona. "Time is limited, and I intend to use it to put some questions to Ms. Cleever."

Next to me, the FBI woman achieved a double sniff. I had a vision of myself slapping down a handful of tissues on the table in front of her and snapping, "For pity's sake, blow your nose!" I refused to surrender to the impulse, looking down the table to catch Cynthia's eye. It would be nice if she appreciated my reserve.

"Of course we can move on," said Byrd, clearly put out by the interruption. With a grunt, he plopped his substantial body in his chair.

Cynthia was watching O'Donnell, so I turned my attention to him too. Flynn was busy murmuring in his ear, and this time O'Donnell responded with a nod, all the while appraising me with narrowed eyes. From his dour expression it appeared I didn't measure up to his specifications for an intelligence agent. Perhaps it was the fact I was blonde and female. Or possibly his conservative religious sensibilities were affronted because I was gay. Or maybe he simply didn't like Aussies.

Convinced that I was ready for anything the American might spring on me, I waited demurely, my hands folded on the table in front of me. And of course, when O'Donnell spoke, it was to ask a question I hadn't anticipated.

"Would you be prepared," he said, fixing me with a flat stare, "to sacrifice your own life if it meant you could kill Red Wolf?"

CHAPTER TWO

The American military aircraft droned across the Pacific, heading for Washington, D.C. Thanks to the depictions in many movies, I'd expected the interior to be Spartan, probably with hard benches bolted along the sides, the exposed ribs of the fuselage showing, and the noise of the engines making it necessary to shout.

Instead, Cynthia and I were in a well-appointed cabin behind the cockpit, sitting in perfectly comfortable seats at a table bolted to the floor. We had a young officer at our service to provide non-alcoholic beverages and adequate, if unexciting, meals.

We weren't the only passengers, but certainly the most casually dressed, with me in jeans and T-shirt, and Cynthia in one of her usual flowing, floral outfits. Across the aisle from us at a similar table sat Lawrence O'Donnell and his hench- man Flynn, both attired in gray suits. Neither had even loosened his tie.

Behind them were two Secret Service agents, twins in identical dark blue suits. They weren't on high alert: one was sleeping with his arms crossed on his chest; the other reading a paperback. I hoped his boss didn't turn around and catch him with it. The very moral Lawrence O'Donnell was unlikely to approve of a Jackie Collins sex-and-serious-money best- seller.

There was a block of unoccupied seats, then in the rear of the cabin sat a couple of uniformed officers, two more civilians in dark suits, and Special Agent Maddie Parkes. She had a pile of folders beside her and a pair of half-glass reading specs perched on the end of her quite elegant nose. She may well have still be snuffling, but if so, the muted din of the engines drowned her out.

Lawrence O'Donnell hadn't looked our way once. As soon as we had taken off he'd opened his briefcase and begun to read through thick bundles of documents, every now and then making a notation with a thick-barreled gold fountain pen. Flynn was tapping away at a laptop. Several times his glance slid over to examine Cynthia and me, as though he expected to catch us doing something untoward.

I hadn't warmed to Lawrence O'Donnell at our first en- counter, and he certainly hadn't warmed to me. At the meet- ing yesterday in ASIO headquarters, his preemptory question about whether I would sacrifice my own life to kill Red Wolf had brought a murmur from others at the table, and a grin from me.

"Am I to be issued with a cyanide capsule to bite down on, after I've accomplished the deed?" I'd inquired.

Clearly not impressed by my attitude, O'Donnell's slash of a mouth had turned down with displeasure. "I don't get what you mean," he'd ground out.

"You seem to be asking me to volunteer for a suicide mission. Frankly, I'm not keen."

He'd clicked his tongue impatiently. "That's not what I meant. It's your level of commitment I'm exploring."

"Total," I'd said cheerfully. "Absolute, utter and complete."

Cynthia had signaled from the other end of the table, indicating I should shut up, but I'd been seriously riled by O'Donnell. Pretending I hadn't noticed her, I went on, "I categorically state, Mr. O'Donnell, that this assignment has my one-hundred-percent commitment. I just don't see why I have to die to prove it. Dying, I'd reckon, would be one-hundred-and-ten-percent commitment, and I'm afraid I'm not up to that."

O'Donnell had given me the kind of glowering look that probably would have his subordinates shaking in their shoes, but I maintained a bland expression. It didn't seem to me likely I was going to be dropped from the assignment. As the only person who had any chance of identifying Red Wolf, the American needed me.

After the meeting I'd had a private audience with O'Donnell, and impressed him even less. His closing words had included the observation that, "loose cannons can destroy even a meticulously planned undertaking," which I took to mean that he had forebodings about my ability to carry out my undercover role. He hadn't spoken to me again. Even when boarding this military plane in Canberra, he'd merely flicked me a cold glance when I'd said a cheery good morning.

"I'd kill for a gin and tonic," Cynthia announced, squinting at the can of Coke in her hand. As usual, she wasn't sitting in a conventional manner, but had assumed what looked like a rather uncomfortable yoga position. She'd taken off her shoes, tucked one leg underneath her, bent the other so her heel was wedged on the seat cushion, then rested her chin on that knee.

She took a sip from the can and wrinkled her nose. "If I

have to drink this sweet stuff, I'd like to improve the flavor with a shot of Bacardi."

"Be brave," I said. "When we get to Washington you can imbibe to your heart's content."

"Easy for you to say. You're barely a social drinker."

Naturally Cynthia had complete information on my habits and idiosyncrasies, so she knew I drank beer at times, occasionally champagne or wine, but alcohol wasn't something I missed if it wasn't available.

"I had no idea you were an alkie," I said, grinning.

"There's a lot you don't know about me."

That was true. It wasn't from lack of trying. I'd admitted to myself long ago that Cynthia quite fascinated me. Among other things, I'd wondered about her sexual orientation, but had never come to any definite opinion on the subject.

Cynthia took another swallow of Coke, grimaced, then flipped open the folder on her lap. "Okay, let's go over your story yet again."

As she'd been doing for weeks, Cynthia peppered me with questions, ready to nail me for any inconsistencies. Who was I? Where was I born? What were the details of my life?

I was Diana Jane Loring, I told her, born in Perth, Western Australia, the illegitimate daughter of Mary Loring.

When my undercover persona had first been discussed, I'd objected to the name *Diana*. "It's just not me," I'd declared.

On previous occasions when I'd been going undercover with a fictitious personality, I'd been able to talk Cynthia around, but this time she'd snapped, "The basic identity's been set up for some time, Denise, waiting for a suitable situation to use it. You're stuck with Diana, so get used to it."

Her ill-tempered response had been out of character, and when I'd looked surprised, she'd apologized. "I've got a lot of people leaning on me," she'd said, "but I shouldn't take it out on you."

Since then I'd realized what she meant. The whole weight of the American intelligence community, personified by

Lawrence O'Donnell, had a big stake in my success in identifying Red Wolf. My preparation had to be perfect, my performance flawless.

I'd immersed myself in the details of the fictional Diana Loring's life. I had to think and behave like someone who had had her experiences — to *be* her. Her name had to be my name, so I automatically responded when anyone used it. Diana Loring had had a hard childhood. Mary Loring had brought me up single-handed, her source of income welfare payments, although she augmented this with occasional prostitution. In my late teens she had conveniently died from a brain hemorrhage.

The official records of the State of Western Australia would show my birth, my spotty education — brought about by our transient lifestyle — my mother's dependence on government handouts, and her occasional arrests for prostitution. There was also a death certificate, indicating my mother had died tragically in the emergency room of a public hospital, victim of a cerebral aneurysm. She been buried as a pauper in an unmarked grave. If anyone checked, it would be as if Mary Loring and her daughter Diana Loring had really existed.

There were further public records to trace Diana's life once she was orphaned. She'd surfaced in Melbourne in her early twenties, when she was arrested at a demonstration against government invasions of personal privacy.

Over the succeeding years my new persona had become a thorough radical, joining various subversive groups, including those whose intent was to undermine the so-called World Government. Fanatical conspiracy theorists maintained there was a nefarious plot to strip individuals of their rights and seize world power. It was claimed this scheme was orchestrated by Zionists, the United Nations, and elements in the judiciary, financial structures and political authorities of Western countries, especially the United States. Successive Australian administrations, so the local conspiracy teaching

13

went, had become lapdogs of the Americans, following whatever secret instructions were dispatched by the traitors of
freedom.

"You speak some Asian languages. How did that come
about?" Cynthia asked.

"I'm lucky enough to be really good at languages. Natural
talent for them."

In reality, this was true. I spoke Japanese and Indonesian
quite fluently, had a good grasp of Thai, and some knowledge
of Vietnamese. English was widely spoken in both Malaysia
and Philippines, but I'd been doing a crash course to gain
some familiarity with Bahasa Melayu, the official language of
the Philippines, and Filipino, that of Indonesia. Apart from
these, years ago at school I'd done basic German and French.
At a push, I could get by in those languages too.

"But why learn them in the first place, Diana?"

The *Diana* still sounded wrong to me, which was a problem. Soon I'd have to respond to it as though it had been my
name since birth.

I grinned at Cynthia. "It was true love that started me off.
I fell in with a group of Asians who'd entered Australia as
overseas students. One was a handsome Indonesian guy I just
couldn't resist, and when I got tired of him I moved on to a
boy from the Philippines. He had the most gorgeous
brown eyes and was a part-time body builder who had ambitions to —"

"Don't embroider, Denise."

"You used my real name." It was rare to catch Cynthia
out, and I enjoyed the moment.

She scowled. "That's because you absolutely drive me mad
with your dangerous tendency to embellish. Just stick to the
Diana Loring narrative we've worked out. All right?"

"Sorry."

Cynthia gave an vexed sigh. "Go on with the story."

"These students I was mixing with were pretty radical, and I got swept up in the whole rebellion against oppressive governments thing. It was only natural I'd start concentrating on Asian languages so I could do my part in liberating South East Asia."

Across the aisle, Flynn was heaving himself out of his seat. He shot me a look of pure dislike. I managed not to take this personally. In our short acquaintance I'd decided Flynn didn't like anyone, other than his boss, and in that case it was brown-nosing, rather than respect or affection. I watched him head for the cockpit and disappear through the door.

"What do you think of Flynn?" I said to Cynthia.

She dismissed him with, "He's a parasite. Now, can we get on?"

We resumed questions and answers. The fictional Diana Loring had specialized in Asian boyfriends, eventually following one to Malaysia, where she'd fallen in with covert groups fighting the government. Escaping capture by the skin of her teeth, she'd fled to neighboring Indonesia, where she'd gone underground with yet another dissident movement.

I went off for a toilet break. When I came back Flynn had reappeared, and was bending over O'Donnell, speaking in urgent tones. After much confidential muttering, Flynn straightened up to signal imperiously at one of the suits sitting at the back of the cabin.

"Something's up," I said.

Flynn and the guy, who was carrying a brown leather folder, went into the cockpit area, closing the door be- hind them. Twenty minutes later, the two of them reappeared to confer with O'Donnell.

This time Flynn beckoned to me.

"Only you," he said when Cynthia went to get up too.

I raised my eyebrows to Cynthia, then obediently moved over to Flynn's side of the cabin.

O'Donnell raised his heavy head to make eye contact with me. "This is Benjamin Attwood," he said. "He'll be briefing you on the latest developments. If you've got questions, he'll answer them."

"Okay," I said agreeably.

Benjamin Attwood was older than I'd first thought — probably in his mid-forties. He had a long face, rather like an anxious llama's, wispy brown hair, and large, lustrous brown eyes. Predictably, he wore the uniform of his fellows — dark suit, white shirt, and plain tie.

"Ma'am, we can sit down over here."

Ma'am? "You can call me Diana," I said, "as I fully intend to call you Ben. Or Bennie, if you'd prefer."

"Ben is fine."

He had a precise way of speaking, as though making sure every word was clearly enunciated into an invisible microphone. I had the disturbing thought that perhaps that wasn't so improbable. Someone like Lawrence O'Donnell invited paranoia. The idea of secret recordings of conversations didn't seem all that far-fetched.

"Are we being recorded?" I asked.

His eyebrows went up. "I don't believe so." He looked at me intently. "Why do you ask?"

"Paranoid delusions." I grinned at him. "Didn't my dossier mention those?"

He played it straight. "I don't recall any such analysis."

I sighed to myself. This guy didn't appear to have any sense of humor. Then again, working for Lawrence O'Donnell probably precluded a sunny attitude to life.

After we were seated opposite each other, a metal table between us, his leather folder in front of him, I said, "It's a spanner in the works, isn't it, being forced to use an Aussie?"

"On occasion we use operatives who are not American citizens." His tone didn't invite any further comment on the matter.

It was plain I wasn't going to entice him into a friendly chat. "I've got a question, Ben."

"Yes?" His tone was cautious, as though he expected me to trick him into some admission.

Indeed, that was my aim. I said, "How many agents have you already planted in SHO?"

SHO stood for the Safe Homes Organization, a group closely affiliated with the militia movement in North America. As the name implied, secure accommodation was provided in major cities for selected political dissidents. A client might be an escapee from Federal detention, someone fearing imminent arrest, or an individual whose unlawful activities demanded a safe, temporary base. This service was not provided free — a considerable payment was required, in advance. Diana Loring had already remitted the designated amount to an off-shore bank in the Cayman Islands.

"None," Ben Attwood said. "You'll be the first."

I'd already asked the same question during an American briefing in Australia, and been given the same answer. I hadn't believed it then, and didn't now.

"How come?" I said, all polite inquiry.

He sat back to consider his answer. "The organization's hard to penetrate. We didn't want to run a chance of tipping them off they were under surveillance. The present situation, however, makes it necessary to insert you."

He flipped open his leather folder. The left side had a clip holding several printed messages. Opposite was a yellow writing pad covered with rows of neat handwriting. I could see that even where he'd crossed something out, it had been done precisely.

Looking up, he gave me the benefit of his sincere brown eyes. I noted his eyelashes were indecently long, quite wasted on a man. "First, SHO has been doing its homework."

"Diana Loring's been checked out?"

Even when he nodded assent, he was well regulated, mak-

17

ing only a minimal movement as he bobbed his head. "SHO initiated a search of Australian records of your cover identity. Similar attempts in the Philippines and Indonesia were less successful, because of the number and variety of the rebel groups. I believe they gained enough, however, to convince them of your veracity."

"So nice to know they're thorough," I said airily.

Attwood's serious expression didn't change. "As you're already aware, the National Security Agency intercepted messages indicating that Red Wolf would be in Los Angeles within the space of four or five weeks."

The NSA used spy satellites and sophisticated antennae to collect, decode and translate telephone, computer, radio and other communications outside the United States. Indeed, Pine Gap in a remote part of the Australian continent was part of the NSA network.

"You've got more up-to-date information?"

Again, an economical bob of his head. "In the last few hours NSA decoded a series of messages that place Red Wolf's arrival in Los Angeles as early as next week."

He was waiting for me to comment, so I said, "That's going to rush things."

"It is. Now we have the proverbial ticking clock in the mix. Clearly there's insufficient time to transport you to Indonesia and have you board a commercial flight to the States as Jenny Philips."

Diana Loring, fictional though she was, appeared on wanted lists in Indonesia, the Philippines and her native Australia. It would be expected that she would travel with false documentation. I was wryly amused with the notion of going undercover while already undercover.

ASIO had wanted to fly me directly from Canberra to Indonesia in a RAAF aircraft, but Lawrence O'Donnell had been very insistent I make the detour of thousands of miles to Washington. He'd claimed it was for further face-to-face briefings that couldn't be accomplished in Australia. It was apparent on our side of the Pacific that the real reason was related to his general distrust of me and my suitability for the part I was to play in fingering Red Wolf.

First, I wasn't an American, so I couldn't be expected to have deep, patriotic feelings for the United States. Apparently my deep, patriotic feelings for Australia carried little weight.

Second, my career as an undercover agent had contained many occasions where circumstances had dictated that I act on my own, take risks, and generally be a one-woman show. This was the antithesis of O'Donnell's idea of how intelligence missions should be carried out. He'd questioned me closely on what he described as my "propensity to act without relying on back-up and team support."

I'd tried arguing with him, pointing out the necessity at times to rely on one's wits and instincts, but he'd remained impervious to persuasion. At first I'd thought O'Donnell too dim to understand the points I was making. Later, I decided he was one of those people who are more than inflexible — their thought processes are set in concrete. Whatever his IQ might be, and I was uncharitably guessing low average, Lawrence O'Donnell always operated on the basis that his opinions and beliefs were inevitably correct. It followed, therefore, anyone who disagreed with him was in error.

I had a strong feeling that O'Donnell was already arranging for me to be vetted by one or more of his people before I would be permitted to go undercover on his turf.

"If there's no time to get me to Jakarta to board the appropriate commercial flight, what happens if SHO checks out the passenger list?"

"We're arranging for someone of your general description to board the plane as Jenny Philips, which is the name SHO will be looking for, but the scheme isn't foolproof, because we don't have time to get someone in place who resembles you very closely. You'll switch with her at LAX after the flight lands."

He shook his head, neatly, of course. "I know it's not ideal, but we're going to have to take the chance it works."

"*I'm* the one taking the chance."

His long face was split with a sudden smile. "Believe me, I appreciate that particular fact, more than you know," he said. "I'm going to be your control."

CHAPTER THREE

"Welcome, Diana. My name's Cheri," she said, shaking my hand firmly. "I'm the resident expert on the Safe Homes Organization."

She wore a dark, tailored dress, had short sandy hair, a pleasant smile, and a purposeful manner.

The windowless, brightly lit room was like being entombed in a clinically white box. The only furniture was a shiny metal table with matching chairs. I returned Cheri's smile. "Would you mind telling me where the hell I am?"

After the plane had landed in mid-morning Cynthia had said, "See you later," and walked off with Lawrence O'Donnell and his entourage toward a low building, I'd been bustled into a generic black car waiting on the tarmac, accompanied by two agents who'd boarded the military aircraft, spoken briefly to O'Donnell, then collected me with such dispatch that I hardly had time to shrug on a denim jacket and grab my cabin luggage.

It was irritating to be treated like a parcel, and even more irritating that neither of the two men in the ubiquitous dark suits responded to my questions about where we were going. Because there'd been an opaque barrier between the passenger section and the driver, and the windows around me were heavily tinted, I saw only vague outlines whizzing by outside. I did get the impression we were in a rural area. After about forty minutes we turned onto what felt like an unmade road, bumped along for about a kilometer, then stopped.

I'd had a quick glimpse of a collection of anonymous, single-story, concrete buildings set in the middle of nowhere, before being whisked inside the largest structure. Then there'd been a short flight of stairs down into the basement, where I'd been delivered to this Cheri, all with barely a word being exchanged.

Cheri grinned. "The boys do love their secrets, don't they? This is a Homeland Security facility. It hasn't always been so, but after 9-11, the buildings were reassigned."

"And what was the facility before?"

Her face closed. "I've no idea."

I'd asked the question to see if there was a limit to what this woman would reveal. Clearly there was.

"I'd like to freshen up," I said.

"Sure." Cheri indicated a door on the other side of the room. "There's the bathroom. We're on rather a tight schedule, I'm afraid. I'm sure you'd like some refreshments, so I'll order coffee and something to eat."

I collected my make-up from my carry-all, which one of my taciturn escorts had deposited just inside the door, and made my way to the austere white bathroom. Apart from the toilet, there was a shower stall — at which I looked longingly — shelving holding folded white towels, and a hand basin with a mirrored cabinet set above it. I checked inside: aspirin, eye-drops, packaged toothbrushes, toothpaste, and several small packets of tissues.

I fished out my own toothbrush, cleaned my teeth, then washed my face with cold water to dispel some of the grubby fatigue I felt. I would have loved a shower, but Cheri's mention of a tight schedule put paid to that idea.

I gave myself a once-over in the mirror. It was plain the application of make-up would be of little use. The signs of jetlag were apparent. My fair hair, usually irrepressible, had lost its spring. I seemed to have developed more subtle facial lines than I recalled. Hopefully, that was the fault of the harsh lighting. My eyes were faintly bloodshot, but nothing like they would have been had I still been wearing contacts. Several months ago I'd had laser eye surgery, so I no longer needed to wear corrective lenses. Diana Loring had been given hazel eyes — a nicely vague term that covered the nondescript greenish-brown color of my own.

I stared at myself, my nose almost touching the mirror's surface. "Ve haff vays of making you talk," I intoned in my best fake German accent. This frivolity didn't ease the tension in my shoulders. It had to be faced: this was a lot more than my normal apprehension at the beginning of a new assignment. This time I was close to being unambiguously scared.

Cheri was waiting with coffee, sweet rolls and truly gigantic biscuits, large as small plates. Pulling out a chair for me, she said, "Have a chocolate-chip cookie. They're delicious, and my great weakness."

She checked her watch, an incongruously lime-green sporting model. "I'm afraid we'll have to hurry along a bit. There are a couple of other people you need to see."

"No doubt I'm being vetted to see if under pressure I run about, frothing at the mouth."

Cheri chuckled. "I'm afraid it is something along those lines, but don't take it personally. It's standard procedure when we bring in someone from outside."

I took a gulp of excellent coffee. "Okay, fire away."

Passing me a manila folder, she said, "Here's back-up material to study at your leisure, including floor plans of the Skinners' house in Beverly Hills and a list of their known associates."

She put a check list on the table in front of her, setting a pen neatly parallel to the page. To avoid repetition, I mentioned I'd already been given the broad details about the organization. Cheri frowned. It was obvious she intended to cover her points in sequence, no matter what prior information I claimed to have.

"We'll start at the top," she said firmly.

First, she outlined the function of SHO, which was to provide safe accommodation for political dissidents who shared the organization's views. SHO also assisted in the provision of false documents for fugitives or those wanting to hide their true identities. "We haven't located all of the safe houses. Three have been detected in Los Angeles, but there may be more."

She consulted her check list, ticked off the first item, then launched into a succinct history of the creation of the Safe Homes Organization, which had originally been an offshoot of the broad, anti-government militia movement. After the terrorist attack on the World Trade Center, the number of armed citizen militias and extremist patriot groups dropped significantly as individuals found patriotic feelings for the United States eclipsed their hatred of the government.

"At the militia movement's height in the mid-nineties," Cheri said, "we had documented evidence of almost nine hundred separate groups. This has now dwindled to a few hundred active groups, but these are hardcore believers, and dangerous because of their fanaticism."

"Are the Skinners members of an established militia group? My briefing in Oz didn't mention it."

"Oz?"

"Australia. Short for."

"I get it." Cheri seemed relieved. Perhaps she'd thought it some classified intelligence term she'd unaccountably missed. "The Skinners?" I prompted.

Jason and Tecla Skinner were to be my hosts in Los Angeles. Members of the clandestine SHO, on the surface they appeared above suspicion, owning a luxurious house in Beverly Hills. Both were gainfully employed, he as an engineer with his own small but very successful industrial laser business, she as a journalist specializing in technological developments.

"Oh, they've far transcended the militia," said Cheri with a cynical smile. "Jason and Tecla possess both money and connections, so look down with scorn on the losers and misfits that formed the majority in the original militia movement. They consider themselves serious players at an international level."

She spoke of the Skinners as though they were personal adversaries. "They've linked up with a number of radical and activist groups and individuals, both here and overseas."

"Cheri, I don't want to waste your time covering old territory. I've already been given a detailed summary of the Skinners and their activities."

"And did you learn that the Skinners actually refer to themselves as counter-government specialists?" Her nostrils, I noted with interest, actually flared.

"I hadn't heard that particular term."

"They also claim to be *patriots*." Cheri's tone was stinging. "Patriots! And they play nursemaid to terrorists. You can see why we've had them under the closest surveillance."

"Really?" I said. "If the Skinners are regarded as such a menace, I'm very surprised at least one intelligence agency hasn't put an operative undercover in the organization."

It was only for an instant, but her face changed. Then she said with warm sincerity, "There's no need to put an agent undercover, as we're monitoring the Skinners comprehensively — telephones, cell phones, e-mails, everything."

"Are they aware they're under this comprehensive surveillance?"

Cheri sat back, obviously considering how to answer this. At last she said, "An agent posing as a window cleaner managed to install several bugs inside the house. Unfortunately the Skinners do a regular sweep, so the bugs were discovered within hours."

"So they're certainly on guard, expecting to be observed."

A shrug. "They're arrogant, think they can beat us at our own game."

This information about the bugs being found was fascinating. If, indeed, another undercover agent had been put in place, it seemed clear the person didn't have the run of the Skinners' home. Otherwise, he or she would have known not to place the bugs, because of the regular electronic sweeps.

"So you're telling me I'll be all on my lonesome?"

"I wouldn't say that," said Cheri, somewhat affronted. "We have several teams in the area twenty-four/seven, primed to move in, if and when required."

"What if I'm shunted off to one of the other safe houses in Los Angeles?"

"It won't happen." Cheri sounded very sure. "The Skinners deal with the cream of the crop, not with second-rate militia members fleeing the law. As far as they're concerned, Diana Loring is a successful urban terrorist wanted by three countries. That would meet their definition of success."

"Red Wolf's a zillion times more important."

"That's why there's no way on earth he's going anywhere but to Beverly Hills." She tapped her checklist, clearly intending to get me back on track. "There's a lot we need to cover."

I had to give it to Cheri. She certainly knew the Skinners inside out. She gave me brief histories of them both, practically from birth until the present, plus detailed psychological profiles, activities on the web — Jason was heavily into cyber-porn — shopping choices, television viewing, prescription medicines taken, sexual preferences — she looked at me sideways, I remained non-committal — concluding with a batch of photographs of the Skinners, their friends and associates.

"Not bad looking," I said, examining a headshot of Jason Skinner. In truth, he was extremely handsome.

"He's had extensive facework," Cheri declared with a sniff.

I examined the photo more closely. "Plastic surgery? Really?"

"Jason Skinner's more conceited than any woman could be. You can use that. His narcissistic personality gives him a grandiose sense of his own importance. With Jason, flattery will get you everywhere."

"What about his wife?"

"Tecla Skinner's into power." Cheri all but sneered. "A charming despot, whose bite is much worse than her bark. She's a controller, who wants to know everything about everything. I suggest you feed that need."

After Cheri finally ticked off every item on her checklist, I was taken to another room to endure a battery of psychological and personality tests. There was nothing I hadn't encountered before. Several times I was tempted to throw in some bizarre response to skew the profile they were busily constructing, but the knowledge they had the results of similar evaluations I'd done in Australia kept me honest.

Then, to my secret astonishment, I was taken into a lab for a lie detector test. I was familiar with the process, although no court in Australia would accept such tests as valid. With a stab of indignation, I wondered why my American intelligence colleagues would subject me to this. And what conceivably could I lie about that was of any significance? Here I was, about to put my neck on the line, yet they were treating me like some sort of criminal.

Still simmering with resentment, I allowed myself to be put in the hot seat. A video camera was set up to focus on my face. "Looking for micro-expressions, are you?" I inquired acerbically.

The technician, a dour individual with a pendulous lower lip, was clearly unimpressed. I gave him a savage grin. "Micro expressions? Infinitesimal changes, usually only detected in slow motion replays, indicating the subject's true response to a question, even if disguised."

He grunted, then proceeded to position the monitors to measure my breathing, galvanic skin conductiveness, blood pressure, and pulse rate.

"I suppose you know the National Academy of Sciences has recently debunked the use of polygraphs," I remarked. "Junk science, I think, was the term used."

Another grunt was my only acknowledgment.

When I was fully hooked up, he broke his silence to say, "You ready?"

"My duplicity's under control. Barely, though."

His lower lip twitched in irritation, which made me feel better. It was unfair to take out my ire on someone who was just doing his job, so I made a mental promise to give exemplary replies.

The technician, who hadn't introduced himself, consulted his paperwork. "Okay, we're starting now."

I knew the drill. He would pause after each answer to check my response. There would be two categories of questions: the first would be innocuous queries, used to establish the parameters of my responses. The second category would present me with questions where I might conceivably lie.

"You were born in Australia?" He had a flat, nasal voice. I agreed I was.

"Your name is Denise Cleever."

"Diana Loring, actually."

The technician sent me a long-suffering look. "Your name is Denise Cleever." His voice had a touch of impatient weariness.

"My name is Denise Cleever."

He droned on. I answered automatically, thinking, *Bloody hell. If this technician knows my real name, who else does? And where's the security in that?*

The same two men turned up to escort me to Washington. This time they were slightly more talkative, introducing themselves as Chuck and Ray, but by this time I was well and truly knackered, and after a few exchanges about Australia — Ray had been to Sydney for the Olympic Games — I dozed off for the rest of the trip.

Our destination in Washington was not the luxury hotel of my dreams. When I voiced my disappointment, Ray, who'd become positively talkative, pointed out it was something almost as good, although lacking room service. Nestled behind wrought iron gates, it looked like an embassy belonging to some particularly prosperous country. In the past, Ray informed me, the building had been shared by various intelligence agencies, mostly for the purpose of stashing important individuals out of harm's way and/or the rapacious eyes of the media. Obviously of the opinion Ray was talking too much, Chuck glared at him. Ray ignored his partner, going on to tell me the building was now, however, exclusively a Homeland Security safe house.

Ray escorted me inside, past armed guards who made no

challenge, obviously recognizing him. Cynthia, showered and refreshed, was waiting. Handing me my bag, Ray intoned that omnipresent American mantra, "Have a nice day."

I responded in my broadest Aussie accent. "Have a bonzer one yourself, mate."

"Making friends with the enemy?" remarked Cynthia as she led me upstairs to my room.

She was being facetious, but there was an element of truth in her description. Intelligence and law enforcement agencies, even those sworn to protect the same country, had frequent and often ferocious turf wars. The problem was magnified when foreign agencies were involved. Australia and the United States were long-term allies on the world stage, and ASIO had entrusted one of their agents — namely me — to America's intelligence network. Of course ASIO would expect some future benefit for this favor. Even so, having an Australian national involved in a perilous assignment on United States soil still wouldn't guarantee that ASIO had any special access to information about this particular assignment.

Cynthia ushered me into a charming, old-fashioned room with floral wallpaper and heavy furniture. "Have a shower and relax. I'll have a tray sent up — comfort food of some sort. Then I suggest you have an early night. You've got an awful lot to fit in tomorrow."

"Like what?"

"Like another meeting with Lawrence O'Donnell, who's apparently taking a keen, personal interest in the whole operation. And a session with the leader of the special operations teams. I'll be liaising — love that word — with Ben Attwood, and then the three of us will go through the protocols one last time before you leave for L.A. midday tomorrow."

"Tomorrow? Jeez! I thought I had another day."

Cynthia patted my hand, though I didn't really need soothing. My complaint was mere self-indulgence, to make up for hours of being psychologically prodded and poked.

"Did you know," I said, tossing my cabin bag on the bed,

"they actually gave me a lie detector test? Asked me all these personal questions about my loyalty to democracy, and if I'd ever revealed national secrets to the enemy, or been blackmailed."

Amused by my indignation, Cynthia said, "You lied, I suppose?"

"My head off. Distorted, prevaricated and equivocated. I was deceit personified."

Cynthia raised one eyebrow, a trick I'd never mastered. "I don't believe you."

"You shouldn't. I'm lying." I smothered a yawn. "Why are things being moved up a day?"

"Lawrence O'Donnell has decided he wants you well in place before the target gets to Los Angeles. It's Wednesday today, and the best information puts Red Wolf in California at the beginning of next week. That means you're to be at LAX tomorrow evening, all ready to become Jenny Philips jetting in from Indonesia."

I perched on the edge of the bed, not daring to sink into one of the seductively upholstered lounge chairs, as I doubted in my present drooping state I'd be able to get to my feet again. "I hope someone's advised the Skinners I'm coming in early."

Cynthia gave me a long-suffering look. "Naturally that's been taken care of with an e-mail originating in Jakarta. A confirmation came back saying you'd be met at LAX. You're to look for a limousine driver holding up your name."

"I can't wait to get this whole thing underway," I said, my eyes watering as I resisted yet another yawn. My tone was flippant, but it was absolutely true. My initial misgivings about this assignment had evolved into a nagging worry, dragging down my usually buoyant spirits. So many things could go wrong.

"I'll send up soup and toasted cheese sandwiches," said Cynthia, moving toward the door.

"What kind of soup?" I asked this automatically, although

31

I didn't really care. My thoughts were snagged in the negative possibilities of the coming assignment.

"Let it be a surprise," said Cynthia, leaving.

I hoped there weren't too many other surprises ahead. If the worst happened, and I was exposed as an undercover agent, what would be explained as an unfortunate failure for national intelligence agencies, would mean for me a certain — and perhaps horribly painful — death.

CHAPTER FOUR

Showered, breakfasted, and in a better frame of mind, I was taken for an audience with Lawrence O'Donnell early the next morning. I was not surprised to learn from his executive assistant, a slight young man so supremely groomed he seemed to have just stepped out of a protective plastic envelope, that O'Donnell routinely arrived before anyone else. It was just the sort of early-bird superiority I would have expected of him.

I expected to be kept waiting, but was ushered into O'Donnell's presence almost immediately. Presence was the right word: he loomed behind a huge mahogany desk, radiating complacent power.

"Sit down," he said, waving his assistant out of the room.

I looked around for Flynn, expecting to see his unappetizing self ensconced somewhere, but we were alone.

Seating myself in a distinctly lesser chair than O'Donnell's massive, black leather one, I said, "Beautiful morning. The sunrise was quite spectacular. But I did think spring would be warmer, here in Washington."

So much for pleasantries. His square, heavy face remained impassive. "I'll be a moment." He returned to the papers in front of him, his fat fountain pen poised to make notations on the pages.

I looked around. The room was paneled with dark wood, making it seem smaller than it actually was. The window had heavy maroon drapes, matching the thick carpet. Several hunting scenes were illuminated by recessed lighting, as was a display case holding an antique musket, a couple of dueling pistols, and a sword half-drawn from its ornate scabbard.

The surface of O'Donnell's desk held three telephones — one undoubtedly a direct line to the White House — and a crystal paperweight with a miniature Stars and Stripes waving within it. Apart from the papers in front of him, the only other items on the desk were two gold-framed photographs, set at an angle so I could see them clearly.

One depicted what was obviously the O'Donnell family, showing a crisp blonde wife with a practiced smile, and two children — the requisite son and daughter — both flashing white, toothy grins. The other gold frame held a striking photograph of a dog.

"What a beautiful golden retriever," I said as O'Donnell capped his pen and leaned back in his chair.

His stolid expression melted into a smile, revealing dental work that lived up to the family's standard of excellence. "That's Rexie," he said, his tone indulgent. "He *is* a fine animal."

O'Donnell's smile hung around for a moment, then disappeared. He tapped the papers in front of him. "Your assessments were e-mailed to me immediately after you completed the testing yesterday."

"I imagine I passed, or you wouldn't be sending me to Los Angeles later today."

He clicked his tongue. "As you're perfectly aware, Ms. Cleever, there's no pass or fail. It's a profile, a tool, and a means to help us all work together with maximum efficiency."

He picked up a page and studied it. "I'm not altogether surprised to find you score low on conformity, and high on initiative." His tone indicated this did not please. "I place a great deal of weight on teamwork."

When I didn't respond, but merely looked politely attentive, he pursed his lips. "Let me be very frank, Ms. Cleever. I'm afraid you would not be my first choice for this assignment."

I had to laugh. "I don't imagine I'd be *any* choice, Mr. O'Donnell, if circumstances hadn't forced you to use me."

He acknowledged this with a slow, deliberate nod. "That's true, but there's no reason to suppose this won't be a successful operation. You've been given the protocol? When you identify Red Wolf, you're to take the first opportunity to advise the leader of our special operations team. From that point it's up to us. Your only responsibility is to stay out of the way. The team will bring the mission to a successful conclusion."

I thought he was being unduly optimistic. "You're describing the best possible scenario. There's always a chance this won't go according to plan."

My remark was clearly unwelcome. "As far as possible you are to follow the guidelines you've been given. Initiative is all very well, but I've got no time for glory seekers."

He paused to make sure I realized I was expected to keep a low profile, and eschew taking credit for the mission's success, then went on, "We each have our role to play. If we all work together appropriately, our objectives should be met."

"Speaking of working together," I said mildly, "you've already got an operative undercover in the Los Angeles SHO organization, haven't you?"

O'Donnell looked at me sharply. "Who told you that?"

"No one told me. It's entirely logical, as the Skinners are potentially so dangerous." I grinned. "And also you'd be wanting to have someone from your side in place to keep an eye on me, wouldn't you? For insurance."

"Insurance?"

"If I do identify Red Wolf, but can't for some reason alert the special operations team, then someone else will be available to assess the situation, and if it calls for it, take Red Wolf out. I'd say that would be your thinking."

A long silence followed. O'Donnell drummed his thick fingers on the desk, his mouth an angry, tight line. "Very well," he said at last, "as I don't want you distracted from your core mission by speculations about who might be a plant, I'll confirm this — we have an operative in SHO. That's all I'll confirm. For security reasons, the identity will not be revealed to you, and you are not to make any attempt to ascertain who it might be."

"What if I'm in a tight spot, and need a friend?"

O'Donnell permitted himself a small, frosty smile. "I have only one piece of advice. Don't get in a tight spot."

A discreet knock on the door, and O'Donnell's assistant appeared. "Sir? It's important." He indicated the white phone on his master's desk.

O'Donnell picked up the receiver, snapped out, "O'Donnell." He listened, his eyes narrowed, rapped out a few sharp questions, and ended with, "Keep me fully informed."

He put down the receiver and turned his attention on me. "Latest intelligence," he said. "The terrorist attack on Los Angeles — we have the objective."

"LAX?" Los Angeles airport, one of the busiest in the world, was a prime target.

"Not the airport. Atomic reactors. There's two of them. Diablo Canyon nuclear plant is on the coast to the north, and

36

San Onofre to the south. Apparently both are targeted. Security upgrades have been ongoing since nine-eleven, but nothing can be made completely invulnerable."

I'd seen a sobering report on nuclear plant vulnerability. Of the hundred and four power plants in the United States, almost half had failed security tests during mock terrorist incidents.

"Any idea on the mode of attack?" I asked, visualizing a plane slamming into the dome of a nuclear power plant, or the sabotaging of the reactor to cause a catastrophic meltdown like that at Chernobyl.

"As yet, we don't have that information." O'Donnell grunted his frustration. "Conceivably the plants could be attacked from sea, air or land."

"How about an inside job?"

"Every single person working at nuclear facilities within the United States has been fully screened."

His positive tone belied a truth we both knew — however intense the screening, there was never any guarantee every individual could be trusted. Indeed, former employees at plants had complained about inadequate training and background checks.

O'Donnell pushed back his chair and stood, leaning his hands on the desk. With his thick neck and brawny body, he looked physically dangerous, but this was of no help when fighting a faceless enemy whose attacks would come at any time, and in any place.

"The National Nuclear Security Administration is sending nuclear emergency teams to L.A.," he said, "and the Department of Health and Human Services is in the process of alerting medical facilities and activating decontamination units."

"It's going to be hard to keep this quiet."

"If word gets out," he said, shaking his head, "there'll be wholesale panic. There are half a million people within ten miles of those two reactors. Potassium iodide pills were distributed months ago to those at greatest risk of exposure, but that's mere window-dressing."

As part of my preparation, I'd studied in detail likely targets in Southern California and the steps to be taken if a terrorist assault took place. If there were to be a major radiation leak, potassium iodide pills had to be taken within four hours of exposure. Even then, these only protected the individual against one type of radioactive isotope absorbed by the thyroid gland. A catastrophic breach of a reactor would spew deadly material into the environment, where wind and water would spread it rapidly. The only protection in this eventuality would be mass evacuations.

"Do you have any indication of when the attack is scheduled?" I asked.

He straightened, moving his shoulders as though his neck was stiff. "Nothing definite. I think we can safely assume it will be after Red Wolf arrives. We have no clear idea of how much of his infrastructure is already in place. He may be ready to move almost immediately."

We looked at each other in silence, contemplating the possibilities. It was a bleakest of pictures. The sheer numbers fleeing from the invisible threat of radiation would generate almost unimaginable traffic problems. There would almost certainly be scenes of frenzied hysteria as panic spread like an infection and people outside the immediate danger zone joined the exodus.

Should the domes of both reactors be breached, initial deaths from radiation would be few, being limited to people working inside or very close to the plants. Within twelve months, however, sixty thousand would die, followed by thirty-five thousand longer-term cancer victims as the years went by. The property damage would be in the billions. And the report I'd read had emphasized that these were conservative figures.

"How reliable's the intelligence you've got on this?" I asked. "Could it be yet another false alarm?"

"The information's rated as high probability," said O'Donnell, "but that doesn't mean it's fully accurate."

He sat down again, wiped his face with his hands. "If we pull all our forces from other areas, patrol the sea and the air, and ring the atomic plants with armed national guards, we can conceivably make those reactors impregnable, at least for the moment."

All major population centers have specific weaknesses, and not enough resources to fully protect all of them. Los Angeles, situated as it was in semi-desert, was dependent on water being piped great distances. Although popular scenarios talked of poisoning water supplies, in reality it would take truckloads of toxins to contaminate a reservoir. Even if this were done, the normal purification procedures would kill biological agents. The real Achilles heel of water utilities was to be found at the pumping stations. Disabling or destroying the series of huge pumps would almost instantly cut off water to much of Los Angeles. And if this coincided with fires set at key spots around the city, a nightmare situation would result.

"Perhaps that's the plan. To draw your resources away from other targets."

"Very possibly." O'Donnell slapped his hand hard on the desktop. "We must be proactive. Stop the attack before it can be launched, whatever the target might be."

There was a sharp knock at the door, and yes-man Flynn bustled in, laptop swinging in one hand. His sparse hair on end, his weak face filled with fervent zeal, he announced, "I came as soon as I heard." When O'Donnell didn't respond, Flynn went on, "Nuclear reactors? It'll be a logistical nightmare." He sounded inordinately pleased with this assessment.

His boss jerked his head in the direction of a chair on the other side of the office. "Sit. Ms. Cleever and I are about to conclude our meeting."

Totally ignoring me, Flynn said, "Will we be going to L.A.?"

O'Donnell's face darkened in a scowl so ferocious that

even I felt taken aback. "My movements are a security matter," he snapped, "and not to be disclosed in front of any third party."

Flynn hesitated for a moment, seeming to decide whether to bolt back out the door, or over to the indicated chair. The chair won. As he sat, he darted a malevolent look at me, apparently considering it my fault he'd been reprimanded.

O'Donnell gathered up the papers in front of him, tapping them against the surface of the desk to square them up. Sounding almost disgusted, he said to me, "I'm very much afraid it's up to you. My hope is you recognize the man the moment you see him, and we neutralize Red Wolf as quickly as possible."

I was about to agree that I desired this fully as much as he, but he went on, "I don't want you to think I'm insensitive to the fact that you're putting yourself in considerable danger."

This concern was a pleasant surprise. I was wondering whether I should modify my opinion of Lawrence O'Donnell when he added, "As a matter of principle, I'm very much against putting young ladies in hazardous situations."

"You were doing so well a moment ago," I said. "And now you've gone and ruined it."

CHAPTER FIVE

I've always hated waiting. Prickling with impatience, I took two strides each way around the cramped little office in the bowels of the international terminal at LAX.

"What if one of the other passengers on the flight from Jakarta become second best friends with my double?" I said. "And then this super-sociable person just happens to notice the Jenny Philips on the flight is not the Jenny Philips who walks up to the limo driver with the sign and says, 'Here I am.' "

"Under control." Maddie Parkes sniffed, then blew her nose. "Hay fever," she added, unnecessarily.

"How is it under control? And I don't mean your hay fever."

"There'll be a terrorist alert on your flight after the plane lands," said Maddie, seeming surprised I wanted the details. "All passengers, including the woman impersonating you, will be channeled off for individual security screening. While this is going on, the switch takes place, you go through immigration and customs, and not until you're well away is anyone else on that flight released."

The FBI agent had been waiting for me when I arrived at the terminal with my two new escorts, Tim and Olivia. I'd traveled from Washington with Ben Attwood and Cynthia in an aircraft masquerading as a cargo plane. We'd landed at LAX and taxied to a remote corner of the airport. There I'd been delivered to Tim and Olivia, who were waiting with a small airport truck. I'd felt rather like a package being passed from one set of couriers to another.

Ben had shaken my hand and wished me good luck. "I'll be waiting for your call, twenty-four hours a day," he said, his long, llama face glowing with earnestness.

Cynthia had alarmed me by giving me a quick hug, a demonstrative act she'd never taken before, no matter how hazardous the mission.

"If I don't make it, Cynthia," I said bravely, "I want a touching memorial service."

"Of course you do."

"And no stinting on the show. White doves are out, because the poor things so often die, but masses of colored balloons released into the sky would be nice."

"They'd be a hazard to aircraft." Cynthia could always be relied on to be practical. Then she'd given me a wicked grin. "And we can't have that when you're sure to be honored with a ceremonial flyby, can we?"

It didn't seem I could indulge in that sort of tension-releasing banter with Maddie Parkes. Perhaps allergies had destroyed her sense of humor. I checked my watch, which had endured a dizzying change of time zones in the last forty-eight hours, and was now showing eight-fifteen in the evening, Los Angeles time.

I was about to ask Olivia and Tim, who were standing guard outside, if anything was happening, when Olivia beat me to it by putting her head through the office door to say, "Okay, folks, listen up. The flight's landed and is taxiing to the terminal."

A surge of excitement and fear rose in my throat. I grabbed my new carry bag, which had been carefully packed with a mixture of articles Diana could have brought from Australia plus things purchased in various places in Indonesia and Malaysia. The clothes I was now wearing, a loose batik top, white cotton pants and sandals, came from small village mar- kets. My suitcase, which was about to be unloaded from the plane's hold, had been packed in Jakarta with a similar blend of Aussie, Malaysian and Indonesian items.

Flanked by Tim and Olivia, and followed by Maddie Parkes, I was swept through a rabbit warren of corridors until we stopped at a door bearing the words, *Strictly No Admittance.* "Wait here," said Tim, opening the door and mo- tioning to me.

Maddie followed me into a cube-shaped little room very similar to the one we'd just left, except it had a second door on the opposite wall through which came the sounds of people moving and talking.

There was a table, two chairs, and a three-drawer metal filing cabinet. Neither of us sat down. Up to this point non- chalant about everything but her susceptibility to allergens, Maddie's face was now showing concern. "Ready? You've got everything, haven't you? And you've been shown how to use them?"

She was referring to three items I'd been given in Washington. The first was a digital camera, so tiny its dimensions allowed it to be disguised as a credit card. There was no zoom or flash, but it could store pictures with a resolution of 1.3 megapixels on its stamp-size memory card. I was entrusted with the task of photographing Red Wolf. If even with our best efforts, the terrorist avoided capture, at least there would be a clear image of his face available.

Also in the guise of a credit card was the second item, a telephone. It had no keyboard, but when activated was programmed to call a sequence of numbers. The first contact would be my control, Ben Attwood. If he failed to answer, my call would be routed to the leader of the special operations teams. If still unanswered, then to Maddie Parkes. In the unlikely event no one took my call, I could activate the sequence again at a later time. It only had a short range, but I'd been assured that Ben and the special ops teams were situated in a rented Beverly Hills house within two blocks of the Skinners' residence.

The last item was the one I had the most reservations about. It was a composite ceramic knife, invisible to security scans. A wicked, thin-bladed weapon, it was concealed inside a black mascara wand. I much preferred firearms, and hoped never to have to use it.

"Well?" said Maddie, clicking her fingernails on the top of the file cabinet.

"You're making me nervous, Maddie."

"Sorry. It's a touch of nicotine withdrawal. I gave up smoking a few days ago."

"You *smoked*?"

She had the grace to blush. "I know, I know. My allergist's been at me for years. Said there was nothing worse, but you know how it is . . ." Dropping this uncomfortable subject, she said, "What did you think of Artie Quillin?"

"Impressive," I said. And he was. A rock-hard face on a rock-hard body. A compact man who gave the impression he could tear you apart with his bare hands, if the notion came to him. Quillin was in charge of the special operations teams that would be poised to act the moment I confirmed Red Wolf's identity.

I'd met Artie Quillin straight after my session with O'Donnell, and spent a couple of intense hours discussing procedures. Quillin had at least a rudimentary sense of humor, because when I'd asked why the special operations teams didn't use the acronym SOT, his mouth had actually curled in a smile. "O'Donnell's teetotal," he'd said, "so no suggestion of alcohol, thank you very much."

Maddie's face had softened. "Artie *is* impressive. That's the right word."

Artie Quillin and *Maddie*? Her tone indicated something was there, at least on her side. Somehow I couldn't picture them together, although Maddie, sinus problems apart, was more than presentable.

"You know him well?"

"Not well enough." Her laugh was almost girlish.

Tim opened the door through which we'd entered. "Here." He handed me already-completed forms required for entry into the United States, a Singapore Airlines in-flight magazine, and tiny pepper and salt shakers the woman impersonating me had souvenired from one of her meals on the plane.

I put the documents with my passport, the magazine and shakers into my bag, zipped it up, and waited for Olivia to come through the other door. As it opened, Maddie sneezed, and through a tissue said, "Good luck."

Olivia and I slipped into the crowded corridor. Most of the people hurrying along looked fatigued and harassed, as well they might, knowing they were heading for the twin hurdles of immigration and customs. A few were smiling, clearly delighted to be in Los Angeles and about to meet friends or relatives. As always, I looked admiringly at those burdened with little kids. Traveling with tired, bored children, or worse, hyper-active ones, seemed to me a Herculean task.

Olivia had dropped way behind me in the stream of

passengers. She was there as back-up, should any problem arise, but would melt into the crowd once I was through into the terminal.

It went like clockwork. I was just another traveler to be processed. There were long queues, as several planes had landed about the same time, but eventually I made it through immigration, collected a trolley, and went to the luggage carousel indicated for my flight. Not surprisingly, as other passengers had been detained in the fake security alert, I was the first there. I hauled off the suitcase that fitted the description I'd been given — dark green with an identifying bright pink ribbon tied to the handle — did a quick check that the name on the luggage tag was indeed Jenny Philips, loaded it onto the trolley and set off for customs. I had nothing to declare. A bored official waved me through, and I was heading for the cacophony of the terminal and the beginning of my life as Diana Loring.

Everywhere around me people were being greeted and embraced. There were several hand-printed signs held aloft by various individuals. I concentrated on the ones dressed as chauffeurs, and found *Philips* almost immediately.

"I'm Jenny Philips," I said to the body-builder holding the sign. The seams of his dark uniform must have been double-sewed to resist the swell of his over-developed muscles. His thatch of dark hair grew so low he had hardly any forehead, and judging from copious black hair on the back of his hands, and showing above the knot of his tie, I reckoned he'd look rather like a gorilla when stripped.

"Gregory," he said in a light tenor voice. "This all you've got?"

He chucked the sign he'd been holding into the nearest rubbish bin, seized the green suitcase as though it weighed nothing, then put a hairy hand out for my carry bag. "Follow me."

The limousine was shiny black duco with even shinier

chrome. Gregory plunked my luggage in the boot, then came round to open a door for me.

"I'll ride in the front with you."

From his expression, this wasn't the thing to do. "Everything's in the back," he said. "Drinks, phone, television."

"Oh, well, in that case . . ."

There was seating for at least eight people. The little television screen showed CNN, but any audio was drowned out by bland elevator music oozing out of several speakers. There was a selection of hard liquor, however I contented myself with a bottle of ginger ale retrieved from a container brimming with crushed ice. The drink was sweet, not with the ginger bite I was used to, but it quenched my thirst.

We escaped the traffic-choked airport area and got onto the 405 freeway, which was crammed both ways, a sea of red tail-lights on our side, and a corresponding sea of white headlights filling the southbound lanes. I wondered, as I often did in heavy traffic, where all these people could possibly be going.

The limo crept along, every now and then getting up to quite a respectable speed, but inevitably slowing down to a crawl soon after. I remembered reading somewhere that the chaos theory had been used in an effort to explain the odd clogging and then freeing of the flow of vehicles on freeways when there was no obvious cause for such variations.

The screen that separated the passenger section from the driver was down, so I said to the back of Gregory's head, "Heavy traffic tonight?"

"Always like this."

"Really? How can you stand it?"

"Used to it."

So much for light conversation. I settled back in the fat leather seat to marshal my thoughts. I'd seen still photographs and covert surveillance videos of Jason and Tecla Skinner, and heard their recorded voices. I'd studied a floor plan of their luxurious house. All the preparation in the world, however, couldn't fully prepare me for the Skinners in the flesh.

Nor was I totally prepared to face Red Wolf. Assuming the intelligence was sound, and he would be in Los Angeles at the time and place specified, there were several questions that couldn't be answered. What if he had changed his appearance so much I couldn't make a definitive identification? What if I simply didn't recognize him when I saw him? What if *he* recognized *me*?

I agreed with ASIO analysts that it was unlikely Red Wolf had seen my face clearly on the catamaran ferry, but maybe he had the information through other channels. Although strenuous efforts were always made to protect the identity of undercover operatives, I still had the nagging worry that perhaps I'd been linked to ASIO some other way. Perhaps there was a detailed description, or even a photograph. It was a depressing fact of life, but some individuals were willing to sell information for money, even in the tightly-screened intelligence community.

The limousine purred down an off-ramp and onto suburban streets. The Skinners' home was situated north of Santa Monica Boulevard in the area known as the Beverly Hills Flats, maybe because this particular part belied the name of Beverly Hills, being flat.

We turned off Santa Monica Boulevard into wide, palmlined streets and impressive mansions. The palms were the truly impressive variety, soaring high into the air and topped with photogenic fronds. The mansions, many concealed behind high walls, exuded money and an indefinable air of being special. It was dark and quiet. There was little traffic, and very few vehicles were parked on the street. Most of the houses had sweeping driveways that could swallow any number of luxury cars.

The Skinners' place was protected by a two-meter stone wall topped by a row of iron spikes. The heavy iron gates each had an elaborate gold heraldic shield. I expected stone lions rampant on each stone gate post, but they were bare of anything but a security camera, which swiveled to turn its eye on us as the limousine glided up to the gates. A pause, then they swung slowly open.

The house behind the wall was brightly lit. Looking at the tall white pillars flanking the grand entrance, I decided its architectural style was *Gone With the Wind* with a touch of modern decadence.

Gregory hopped out immediately, rushing to open my door before I could. He was unloading my things from the limo's boot when the massive front door opened.

"Diana! Did you have a good flight?"

The woman wore a simple black dress, high heels, and jade pendant earrings. Her smile was more than warm — it was incandescent. Tecla Skinner and I might have been friends for years, rather than total strangers.

"The flight was fine," I said politely.

Gregory deposited my luggage inside the door, then came back to us, the deference in his bearing indicating the respect he had for Tecla Skinner.

She looked him over approvingly. "Thank you, Gregory, that will be all tonight. And please thank Mr. Hydesmith too. Tell him I'll call tomorrow morning."

"Will do."

Hydesmith? I ran a quick mental check of the Skinners' known associates. Edward Hydesmith was extremely rich, and very secretive. He'd made his fortune in judicious real estate purchases, mostly tracts of apparently worthless land on the fringes of cities, which were miraculously cleared by local government bodies for commercial and residential use once he'd purchased them.

Tecla and I stood together until the limousine's tail-lights disappeared, then she linked arms with me and turned toward the house. "You must be tired after that long trip."

I murmured something appropriate, thinking how photographs, and even videos, so often failed to capture the real person. I'd thought Tecla Skinner plain, but now that I had her living self before me, I saw how wrong I'd been. She was one of those rare people possessed of a radiant personality that so suffused her unremarkable features that she gave the impression of being magnetically attractive. And she'd done her best to augment that impression. Her glossy brown hair was beautifully styled, her makeup impeccable, her figure trim. I didn't have to check to know her crimson nails would not have a single chip.

"Jason," she said to the man who'd appeared at the door, "our guest has arrived."

The photos hadn't lied about Jason Skinner. He was almost unrealistically good-looking, with a strong chin (Cheri had remarked he'd had a chin implant), an elegant, high-bridged nose, and dark hair artfully tousled. Revealing a compact body obviously accustomed to many hard hours in a gym, his tight green T-shirt also picked up the intense green of his eyes. This perfection came in scaled-down form, however. Jason Skinner was noticeably shorter than his wife, and therefore considerably below my height.

"Let me get your things." He grabbed my suitcase and bag, leading the way into a splendid entrance area. The floor was pale gray marble, and in the center sat a glossy black table holding an ebony vase filled with glowing red roses. The walls soared two stories to a clerestory which in daytime would flood the place with light. There was the obligatory wide, curved staircase with carved banisters down which one could make a satisfyingly dramatic entry.

"Just a little matter," said Tecla, putting out a perfectly manicured hand. "Your passport, please. Jason will put it in the safe. And about your other things — I do hope you won't mind, but it's a rule we have that we examine everything a guest brings into the house. It includes, I'm afraid, scanning your body with a security wand."

"I've got two passports," I said. "One is in Jenny Philips's name, the other's my genuine passport."

"I'll take them both," she said, smiling. "Don't worry, they'll be completely secure, along with any other valuables you might have. Jewelry, perhaps?"

"I travel light."

Jason made an approving sound. "An excellent idea," he said, casting a meaningful look in Tecla's direction. "Unfortunately it's never been one of my wife's ambitions. She believes in packing at least two outfits for every occasion."

"Don't listen to Jason," she chuckled. "He's the clothes horse in the family."

"That's clearly a slanderous statement."

The repartee was all very charming, but it was also unnerving. These kittens would turn into tigers in an instant if they penetrated my cover.

CHAPTER SIX

I'd left the curtains open in my bedroom, and so was awakened next morning by sunlight falling on my face. I rolled over and stared at the ceiling. Although I hadn't expected to sleep soundly, I had. Yesterday had been long and tiring. The tension generated by the Skinners' search of my things last night had almost depleted the last of my energy.

As Tecla and Jason had gone through my belongings I'd been outwardly calm, but showing, I thought, just the right touch of exasperation at this unexpected examination of my possessions. Inwardly, I was quaking, waiting to see if the devices I had with me would be discovered.

"Credit cards?" Tecla had said, opening my wallet.

"They're both in the name of Jenny Philips, and not bad

fakes," I'd said, praying she wouldn't examine them closely. "They're only for emergencies, as Jenny Philips is a pretty flimsy cover. I expect to use cash until you arrange my new identity. You'll find five thousand dollars in the bottom of my suitcase."

Fortunately, the long flight from Indonesia explained my extreme fatigue. Tecla had taken me up the curved staircase to a guest suite as lavish as any five star hotel could provide.

Her parting words had been disturbing. "It may be a little inconvenient," she'd said, "but we don't allow any calls to be made from the house. You'll find our phones inoperable without the correct code. If you have an emergency, of course something can be arranged. I notice you don't have a cell phone with you, but please don't think of borrowing one to make a call. Our whole property is electronically monitored."

Stifling a yawn, I'd said, "You don't trust your guests?"

She'd smiled. "Precautions have to be taken."

After advising me a buffet breakfast was served every morning in the dining room, she'd left me blessedly alone.

This morning the view from my window confirmed it was a beautiful spring day in California. I made my bed, suspecting that if I didn't, the housekeeper I knew the Skinners employed would do it for me. Then I showered, put on jeans and a red shirt — for good luck in my quest for Red Wolf — and after peering out the window to admire the dancing reflections on the aquamarine swimming pool below, I set off to locate the dining room. I knew exactly where it was from the floor plans I'd seen, but acted appropriately lost until a woman in a black dress and white apron came across me.

"You're looking for breakfast? It's this way."

She was Carmina Hernandez, a Mexican citizen, legally resident in the States. The FBI and INS had fine-tooth combed her background and found nothing amiss. She had been widowed fifteen years ago, and brought up two children on her own. She'd been the Skinners' housekeeper for eight years.

During my briefing Cheri had told me there'd been an ongoing argument about whether to approach Carmina Hernandez to sound her out as a possible source of information about her employers, but it had been decided the risk she might alert the Skinners was too great.

"Hi," I said. "I'm Diana. And you . . . ?"

"Please call me Carmina." Her accent was light, giving a charming flavor to her words.

She ushered me through double doors to an elegant room. No one else was there, but five places were set at the table.

Carmina asked, "Would you prefer coffee or tea?"

I'd had nasty experiences with tea in America — the concept that it *must* be made with water on the boil was not well established — but I was game to try again. "Tea, please, as long as it's genuine, and not that flavored stuff."

Her severe expression relaxed into a smile. "It's Twinings Orange Pekoe," she said. "I'll make a fresh pot for you." She gestured toward the laden sideboard. "Help yourself. There's orange or apple juice. Also fruit, cereal, eggs, bacon, sausages, fried tomatoes, hash browns . . ."

Feeling rather like I'd wandered onto the set for some posh English movie, I took a plate and made a hearty selection. Perhaps I should wait for someone else to turn up? A protest from my stomach decided me it was easier to give in and let hunger get the best of me.

I had just taken my first mouthful when a voice behind me said, "You're wearing red. Red stands for power — and passion."

My pulse jumped. Although the terrorist wasn't supposed to be in L.A. yet, I knew for reasons of added security a change in planned arrival time was likely. This slender man, however, was familiar from photographs. Tecla's brother. He wore the kind of casual clothes — linen pants and a silky knit top — that male models sported on billboards. The word that came to me immediately was *effete*. He drifted languidly across the room and slid into a chair at the head of the table.

He cocked his head. "You must be Diana."

"That's me." I raised my eyebrows in a silent query.

"Innis Cady." He pronounced his name with respect, as though its cadence was worthy of note.

"Innis? Unusual name."

"I chose it. Originally, I was called Bruce." He wrinkled his nose. "Unconscionable, isn't it, to call someone Bruce? Too close to *bruise*, don't you think?" He added, straight-faced, "It's a good thing my parents are dead, or I'd be forced to sue them."

I was diplomatic. "Innis is certainly more interesting than Bruce."

Carmina silently appeared with a silver teapot, poured me a cup and set it beside me.

Although the coffee pot was on the table within easy reach, Innis said in doleful tones, "Carmina, I need coffee desperately."

Plainly accustomed to this calculated helplessness, Carmina got him his coffee, and even put three lumps of sugar into the cup. I almost expected Innis to have her stir it for him, but he did that himself, albeit listlessly.

I looked after Carmina as she left the room. What would it be like to have servants? So much privacy had to be sacrificed. No wonder there'd been heated debate about approaching Carmina Hernandez. Servants were in a unique position to know intensely personal details, as certain high-profile people had found to their cost when tell-all books appeared.

Having stirred his coffee to his satisfaction, Innis put down the spoon and took a sip. He put the cup down with precise care, and asked, "Is Diana your real name?"

"It's my real name." I couldn't resist adding, "I'm quite happy with it."

"We get so many people here who use pseudonyms."

I was wondering how I could turn this subject to my advantage when there was a clack of heels, and Tecla, wearing a filmy housecoat and backless mules, sailed into the room.

55

"Hello, Innis. Diana, you slept well?"

"Thank you, I did."

"Diana is using her real name," Innis observed, his tone suggesting he considered this unusual.

"Not all the time," I protested. "I did enter the country as Jenny Philips, and I'll leave it as someone else again."

"Names are important," said Innis. "Make sure my sister gives you a good one." He regarded me reflectively. "A blond name, I think, something Nordic or Germanic."

Tecla got herself a glass of orange juice, heaped a plate high with sliced melon, and clacked her way over to the table. "Changing one's identity is often a necessary evil. The first defense against a government gone mad."

Her brother groaned. "Now you've set her off," he said to me, quite unjustly. "Any minute now Tecla will be telling you how we're all under surveillance."

"It's no joking matter, Innis." She fixed me with an intense stare. "We have the house swept regularly for bugs."

"Find any?"

"Yes, of course. And there's a tap on our phone, too."

"No!" I said, as astonished as I thought Diana Loring should be. "You're kidding. Who bugged you?"

"The FBI. Perhaps you've heard of the latest outrage? The Federal Bureau of Investigations" — she spat out the title — "has now been authorized to spy on citizens belonging to groups without having the inconvenience of having to prove there's evidence of any crime. Agents can collect information anywhere and everywhere. Internet sites, public meetings, religious congregations."

She paused to let the magnitude of this sink in. "You see where this leads, Diana? The FBI has been given a mandate to discredit, disrupt and otherwise destroy political and activist groups."

With disdain she added, "Land of the free! That's what the

56

majority believe. But the United States is well on the way to becoming a police state, beholden to shadowy figures who hide behind the scenes and pull the strings."

Innis leaned back and laced his fingers behind his head. "I told you not to get her started."

I frowned at his sister. "Tecla, I thought this place was *safe*. If they're bugging you, well . . ." I threw up my hands in a what-to-do gesture.

"Relax," Tecla commanded. She gave me a mischievous smile. "The FBI and the rest of those intelligence clowns know only what we want them to know."

"What do you mean?"

Tecla raised an admonishing finger. "All in good time, Diana. Just be assured that everything's under control."

"Well, okay . . ." I said, clearly conveying I wasn't convinced.

"They're fools, the lot of them," said Innis, rocking back so his chair teetered on two legs. "Surely you've seen stuff, even in the Indonesian media, about American intelligence agencies? The CIA continually mess up big time, and FBI agents can't even find terrorists right under their noses." He snorted derisively. "And as for the Homeland Security bunch, they're running around with their heads up their asses."

Tecla drained the last of her orange juice and put the tumbler down on the table with a decisive thud. "Money, ideals, and the determination to succeed," she said, "will beat any bloated bureaucracy every time."

"For my country," said her brother, raising his coffee cup in a salute.

"For my country," she echoed.

"For my country," said Jason from the doorway.

I was feeling somewhat left out. Should I be raising my apple juice and saluting Australia at this point?

The harsher illumination of daylight did not take the edge

off Jason's good looks. He sauntered over and rested his hand on the back of my chair. Leaning over me he said, "And how are you this morning, Diana?"

His face was so close to mine I couldn't focus on his masculine beauty, but I could smell the astringent tang of his aftershave. "I'm terrific, Jason. How about you?"

"Why, I'm just great." He slid his hand onto my shoulder and squeezed gently. "You've seen the pool? How about a dip before lunch?"

I looked down the table to see how Tecla was taking her husband's over-familiar behavior. She was, to my dismay, smiling approval.

Yikes, I thought, there's something going on here, and I hope it isn't what I think it is.

Innis was commissioned to give me a tour of the property. The building certainly deserved to be described as a mansion. I'd found my bedroom suite luxury itself, and Innis assured me the other four bedrooms in the main house each had its own bathroom and dressing room. "Although the master bedroom is something else again," he remarked. "His and her walk-in closets, a sunken bathtub . . ."

Carmina Hernandez had a separate apartment on the ground floor near the kitchen, which itself was state-of-the-art. I knew from the plans I studied there was another separate apartment upstairs with its own private entrance, but Innis didn't mention this.

Next he showed me around the media center, which comprised a TV room featuring a huge flat screen, a computer room set up with monitors, printers, and scanners, and a mini-theater for screening movies. Apart from the dining room, which I'd already seen, there was an area set aside for entertaining, furnished with sumptuous sofas and lounge chairs and with a bar big enough to cater to the thirst of a multitude of guests. The basement held a full-size billiard table and a well-equipped home gym. Innis didn't mention it, but from the floor plans I'd seen I knew the red metal door in one wall of the basement led to the central security system for the house.

"And now for a tour of the grounds," Innis said grandly as he led me outside. It was close to a perfect spring morning. For a moment I forgot who I was and why I was here. Above the sky was deep blue without a hint of smog, the sun was a warm caress, and a tiny hummingbird, not much larger than my thumb, zipped by.

The large pool of blue-green water was made for swimming, not just splashing around. There was a diving board at the deeper end. Bubbling quietly to itself, the adjacent spa pool could hold six or seven people. A table held folded towels and terry-toweling robes. White furniture, shaded by huge aquamarine umbrellas, contrasted nicely with the expanse of terracotta tiling. Bordering two sides of the area were four cabanas, painted in the earth colors of Spanish architecture. An excellent landscape gardener had been at work, creating a lovely backdrop of palms and bright blooming shrubs. In one corner a barbecue area had been set up.

"Pity Tecla didn't put you in one of these guest houses," said Innis. "You could join me every morning for a quick swim before breakfast."

"I can probably just about manage the trek from the house."

Innis grinned at my dry tone. "We've got two more people coming today who'll be staying out here in the guest houses, but there'll still be one free, if you change your mind." He pointed to the cabana closest to the main house. "That's mine. Care to see it?"

"Did you do this yourself?" I asked when he ushered me through the brass-studded door.

He surveyed the room with satisfaction. "I did."

Innis had kept to the Spanish theme. The walls were stark

white plaster, the floor polished wood strewn with a few bright rugs. The sparse furniture was plain and dark. A small but exquisite Madonna and Child glowed on the wall above an open fireplace.

"That's beautiful," I said.

"I'm not the slightest religious," Innis assured me, "so it was entirely an aesthetic decision."

His bedroom was also minimalist, holding only a king-size bed with a dull red spread, a bedside table and a wardrobe, both of wood stained so dark it was nearly black. I went over to look out the window. Luxuriant foliage partly hid a high metal fence that separated the Skinners' house from the neighbor's place. I visualized the plans — this would be the southern boundary of the property.

Innis said, "Bedrooms tell so much about a person, don't they?"

"Perhaps."

He shook his head. "Such prevarication. And I took you for such a positive person." Smiling slightly, he folded his arms and leaned with casual elegance against the wardrobe. "May I ask you a personal question?"

"And if I say no?"

"I'll ask it anyway."

"I'm bracing myself," I said, curious to see what he would say.

"I was wondering, do you swing both ways?"

"Pardon?"

He gave a soft laugh. "I believe you heard me, Diana."

"Are you going to inquire if I'm into bestiality too?"

"I hadn't thought to, but if you want to tell me . . ."

Diana Loring's sexual inclinations had been presented as heterosexual, as indicated by her relationship with her Indonesian boyfriend. I supposed, when I thought about it, that the canvas was essentially blank for Diana. Who knows what high-jinx she could have got up to in the steamy jungles of Indonesia?

"Nice try," I said, "but I would have to know you a lot better, Innis, before I'd discuss the subject."

"Here you both are!" With one sweeping glance, Tecla took in our relative positions, Innis leaning against the wardrobe, me by the window.

Her brother spread his hands. "I was attempting to entice Diana into my bed."

"With conspicuous little success, I see."

She'd changed into a bright blue swimming costume, over which she wore a paler blue robe. Smiling warmly at me, she said, "I'm here to entice you into the pool. Let me show you the changing room. There's a selection of swimsuits for guests." She looked me up and down. "I'm sure you'll find something suitable."

I agreed to her suggestion with alacrity. I loved the water, and tried to swim laps every day. It was for me the most wonderful relaxation, where the rhythm of my breathing and the repetition of movements put me into something close to a meditative state.

Ten minutes later I was in a black two-piece and contemplating the scintillating surface of the pool. Innis had disappeared, but Tecla had settled herself on a white lounge. The table beside her held a bottle of sunscreen, a fat paperback novel, a dish of mixed nuts, a packet of cigarettes, and a red ceramic ashtray with matching lighter.

She was eyeing me with what I considered a little too much interest, when Carmina appeared with a tray of drinks, each with a bright red, green or purple umbrella.

"We use an umbrella code," said Tecla. "The purple ones are pina coladas, the red margaritas."

"And the green?"

"Non-alcoholic fruit punch, but I wouldn't advise it. Too boring."

I took a glass with a green umbrella. Tecla chuckled. "It's clear you don't take instruction well." She selected a glass with a purple umbrella, and leaned back with a sigh of pleasure. "I hope I can tempt you with something stronger tonight. Two more house guests are arriving today. To celebrate, we're having a dinner party."

Would my quarry be one of the two? Red Wolf at a dinner party . . . I tried to imagine him formally dressed. The only time I'd seen him he'd been wearing a creased khaki shirt and pants, both stained with water.

"That sounds great, Tecla, but I don't have much to wear." She already knew that, having searched my luggage.

"I noticed you did have a black skirt. You're welcome to have a look in my closet for a top, if you wish."

There was one tailored jacket packed for me that would be suitable, but the opportunity to look around the Skinners' bedroom was too tempting. "Thank you," I said. "I'd like that."

A helicopter flew overhead. Squinting, I could make out the logo of a TV station.

"Surveillance," said Tecla.

"It belongs to a television station. Channel Seven."

Tecla snorted. "That's what they want you to think."

I put down my fruit punch. "I'm going to swim a few laps."

"Laps? You take your swimming seriously." Tecla gave me an appreciative glance. "I can see you keep yourself fit."

"I try," I said modestly, amused to think of her reaction if she learned that my regimen had recently included Krav Maga, the Israeli army's self-defense system of kicks, punches, and elbow and knee strikes, all delivered in stunningly fast combinations.

Tecla stripped the cellophane off her packet of cigarettes, selected one, and reached for the lighter. "You don't smoke, I suppose."

"Never have."

"Lucky you." She tilted her head to blow a stream of smoke into the air. "I'm addicted to a couple of things, and nicotine is one of them."

Her sly smile was my prompt to slide into the pool. The

water was deliciously cool against my skin. I swam one leisurely lap, finding that although I would be able to do a fast tumble turn at the deep end, at the other I would have to touch the side. I had a personal rule never to cheat by failing to start and end laps properly.

Soon I was set in a pleasing rhythm, the laps ticking off in my head in a soothing mantra. I was aware that Innis had joined his sister. I could hear the ebb and flow of their conversation, and Tecla's light laugh, but otherwise I was secure in my separate domain where time had collapsed into a tranquilizing sequence of programmed movements.

I'd done twenty smooth laps when I caught sight of Jason's tanned legs out of the corner of my eye. He was standing on the side of the pool, hands on hips, gazing down at me, wearing the briefest possible swimming costume of electric blue. Someone was beside him. I completed lap twenty-one, then came to a stop at the deep end.

Treading water, I glanced in Jason's direction. The woman beside him had a mane of chestnut hair that shone in the sunlight. My heart gave a sickening leap.

It can't be, said an inner voice.

I took a few lazy strokes toward them, willing my racing pulse to slow.

The light refracting on the water dazzled me, so when I arrived at the side of the pool I had to squint up at their looming shapes.

It is.

"Hi, Jason," I said. "Come on in, the water's fine."

CHAPTER SEVEN

"Diana, this is Natalie." Jason took the opportunity to slip an arm around her waist. "Natalie, meet Diana."

I climbed out of the pool. "Hi," I said again, sounding polite but not particularly interested, as I looked into her high-cheeked, familiar face. She appeared tired, and the clothes she wore — a white T-shirt and canvas pants — looked anything but crisp.

What the hell are you doing here, Siobhan?

It seemed certain she was thinking something along the same lines, but in her cool English voice she said, "Nice to meet you, Diana," then turned away to say something to Tecla.

Jason dropped his arm from her waist and hastened to

hand me a super-size towel. He gave me an unmistakably admiring once-over. "Surely you're not getting out of the water yet. I was just about to come in."

I blotted my hair. "Later, maybe," I said, even in my consternation finding myself repressing a smile at his peacock ways. Jason displayed a nice body in a miniscule swimming costume, there was no argument about that, but he was so obviously posing it to best advantage that I was amused, rather than impressed.

The half-full glass of fruit punch I'd left had been taken away, so took I new one from the fresh tray of drinks, spread my towel, and settled down on a lounge next to Tecla. Nearby, Innis, who was lying face down on a towel in the sun to catch up on his tan, appeared to be asleep. I sipped my drink and watched Jason preen before diving into the water with a somewhat inelegant splash.

Listening to Siobhan's delightful English voice, I forced myself to think of her as Natalie.

Natalie was saying, "Nothing's gone smoothly today, Tecla. The border was a nightmare, then the traffic in San Diego and all the way up the coast was diabolical."

Tecla's expression was properly sympathetic. "Crossing from Mexico can be hell, especially since security's been tightened. I always maintain coming in from Canada is much easier. The border's five-and-a-half thousand miles long, and though the Canadians swear there's now round-the-clock surveillance at every remote crossing, it simply isn't true."

"I *was* coming from South America."

"True," Tecla conceded, "but in my view it's worth the extra trouble to fly into Canada, just for the convenience of a porous border." She flashed me a brilliant smile. "And what do *you* think, Diana?"

I shrugged. "You're the expert, Tecla, not me. Now if you were asking about Australia, or South East Asia, then I might have something to say . . ."

So far Natalie and I had managed to convey to each other

only a few generalities about our assumed identities. It was dangerous to be more specific. Somehow I had to speak with her, alone.

It turned out to be my day for introductions. Carmina appeared to ask when lunch was to be served, and Tecla announced we'd be eating early. Innis, who'd turned over to baste his front, grumbled good-naturedly at this, winked at me, and wandered off to his quarters to change. Jason, who'd become bored with swimming solo, and had come over to join in the conversation, suddenly leapt to his feet.

"Vin!"

I supposed this was the other person who'd be staying in one of the guest houses. My skin prickled, but a quick glance told me it wasn't Red Wolf. This man was taller, with distinctive features. His face was gaunt, his nose magnificently hooked. He had straight, dark hair streaked with gray. I figured he was going for an impression of rumpled imperturbability, wearing a suit I'd say was Armani or an excellent knock-off. His white shirt was tieless, and he had a silver earring in one ear.

"Hello, Jason." This was said without the slightest hint of enthusiasm. Vin's smile appeared, however, when he saw Natalie. "You made it, then?"

She laughed. "Clearly, I did."

"It's rare for anything we arrange to go any way but smoothly," said Jason with a complacent smile.

The man's lip didn't actually curl in a sneer, but it was a close thing. Evidently feeling at a disadvantage in his semi-naked state, Jason snatched up a terry toweling robe and hastily put it on. "Vin, this is Diana. I told you all about her."

Vin inclined his head in the manner of a superior meeting a decided inferior, but his words were banal enough. He told me he was pleased to meet me and remarked it was a beautiful day. What was disconcerting was that he spoke in Indonesian. A test? Or merely showing off?

I replied in the same language, commenting rather gracefully, I thought, on the pleasures of a spring day in Los Angeles, especially in these splendid surroundings. I added, with a modicum of surprise, how I'd not expected to hear Indonesian spoken here.

Tecla, who'd watched our conversation with keen interest, broke in with, "You can't continue to chatter away in a language nobody else understands." Favoring us both with her trademark incandescent smile, she added, "We'll all be convinced you're talking about us!"

Vin's expression indicated he wouldn't waste the time. Still speaking Indonesian, he said, "Where were you? Java? Sumatra?" His accent wasn't bad, but there was a definite cadence, not American. I couldn't place what nationality he was.

"This is a quiz?" I said in English. "Do I get a prize if I answer correctly?"

"When I heard you spoke Indonesian, I took it as an opportunity to brush up on my skills."

"I speak several languages," I said immodestly. "Do you?"

I'd managed to irritate him. This time the sneer did make a brief appearance. "I get by," he said.

"Lunch in twenty minutes," Tecla announced, all but clapping her hands to bring us to order. Innis appeared, properly attired, and was dispatched to bring Natalie and Vin's luggage out to the guest houses, so they could freshen up.

"Have you checked out *their* luggage?" I asked Tecla, as Innis reappeared laden with nondescript overnight bags.

"Of course. We make no exceptions." She gave me a tight smile. "It's how we've survived in a dangerous world."

I went upstairs to change, wondering as I did so just how accurate that list of Skinner associates had been. I couldn't recall a Vin or Vincent, either as a first or last name. Nor was there a Natalie.

One reassuring thing occurred at lunch: someone most definitely on the list appeared. Like breakfast, lunch had been set up as a buffet, with an enticing display of salads, meats and shellfish. "Everyone, I think, knows Gail," Tecla said, "except you, Diana."

We murmured desultory words as we were introduced, then Gail Jones, as I knew her to be, turned away to chat with Jason. The photograph in the file had been a good likeness. Gail was stocky, nondescript, and somehow slightly out of focus, as if her doughy face had blurred slightly. Her long, mouse-brown hair flopped dispiritedly on her rounded shoulders. The thing that struck me most about her was her buck teeth, probably because she was so obvious an exception to the surrounding perfect-teeth syndrome.

I reviewed what I knew about Gail Jones. She'd come from a dissident group in New York State, and had been an assistant of Tecla's in Los Angeles for the past two years. I recalled that a handwritten note next to her name had observed that she was, "fanatically loyal."

Lunch was quite informal, with people sitting at the dining table, or wandering out onto the adjoining patio. All that swimming had made me ravenous, so I loaded up a plate with a generous selection and looked around for somewhere to sit. What I wanted most urgently was to talk with Natalie, but it was vital to strike a balance between chatting naturally, as though we'd just met, and showing too much interest in her.

Along with Innis and Jason, Natalie had chosen the patio, and was seated with Vin in animated conversation. They seemed to know each other well, and it crossed my mind that he, too, could be an undercover plant. I was in the midst of strategizing how to casually join them, when Gail Jones tapped me on the shoulder. "Tecla wants you." She jerked her head. "Inside."

Tecla, seated at the dining table, was looking grave. Without her usual animation, her face became commonplace, unremarkable. Innis stood behind her chair, hands in pockets. Gail had followed me inside, and hovered off to my right.

I plunked myself down in an empty seat beside Tecla, took a forkful of potato salad to fortify me, and asked, "What's the prob?"

"The problem, Diana," Tecla said. "is that Carmina has found something rather disturbing in your things."

"Carmina? She's been in my room?"

"Of course. To make your bed and tidy up."

"I made my own bed."

Tecla didn't congratulate me on my thoughtfulness. She placed on the table between us an incongruous item. My mascara wand. And the thin blade it held had been partly withdrawn.

"Well?" said Tecla, "what have you to say for yourself?"

CHAPTER EIGHT

"Neat, isn't it?" I said, silently cursing that I'd failed to give weight to my initial misgivings in Washington, and refused to carry this concealed weapon. "I bought it at a native market outside Kuala Lumpur."

ASIO instructors had spent a great deal of time emphasizing that in situations like this I should avoid giving too much unsolicited detail, because over-explanation caused suspicion, nevertheless I heard myself add, "The market had quite a selection, with rapiers disguised as walking sticks, switchblade knives pretending to be pens — all that sort of stuff. I liked this one, though. Small and insignificant, though I suppose it could kill if you hit the right spot."

Shut up, Denise!

I forced myself to take another mouthful from my plate, although my appetite had entirely disappeared.

Innis leaned over and picked up the mascara wand. He slid the little blade out completely and tested its point against his finger. A spot of blood sprang up. "Jesus," he said, "it's sharp."

"Well, of course," I said. "What would be the use, otherwise?"

"Oh, give me that, Innis," said Tecla, her face lit by an indulgent smile, "before you really hurt yourself."

I thought it time to take the initiative. "What in the hell was Carmina doing in my makeup, anyway?"

"I asked her to check it out." Tecla looked cat-with-canary pleased with herself. "In case you're wondering why, the fact is, I notice details."

Innis nodded agreement. "She does. Eagle eye. Hopeless to try and fool her." Gail Jones bobbed her head in confirmation of this evaluation.

Tecla paid no attention to this endorsement. Indicating the wand, she said, "I saw this last night, when we were checking through your luggage. It was only this morning it occurred to me it was quite the wrong color. You're blonde. It's quite impossible that you'd be using black mascara."

As if she were speaking in my head, I could hear Cheri's description of Tecla: *She's a controller, who wants to know everything about everything. I suggest you feed that need.*

Assuming a contrite expression, I said, "I should have told you I was carrying a weapon, Tecla. Truth is, I was a bit embarrassed. I mean, it seems so ridiculous to be running around with a mascara wand that doubles as a dagger — and a pretty ineffectual one at that, I'd say."

Tecla held the blade up to the light to examine it. "Not so ineffectual. This has its uses — driven into an eye or eardrum, inserted between the vertebrae of the neck, slipping through ribs into the heart, or even puncturing a lung several times." She grinned at me. "Any of the above should do it."

Of course she was right, but as Diana Loring wasn't supposed to be an expert in hand-to-hand combat, I looked impressed. "How do you know all that? I reckon, if I ever had to use that little thing, I'd just stab away at whatever bit was closest."

"Eww," said Gail, wrinkling her nose. Possibly she was turned off by violence in general, but I fancied her distaste was in response to my stated stab-early-and-often strategy.

Tecla fitted the slender blade back into the wand and handed it to me. "You never know when you might need it." She tilted her head, regarding me closely. "Any other secrets, Diana?"

"Only one."

She raised a perfectly groomed eyebrow. "And that would be?"

"Black mascara. I know I shouldn't have, but I've worn it in the past. No more. I've seen the error of my ways."

After lunch Tecla announced we had free time until this evening, when we were expected to turn up for pre-dinner drinks at seven. "And don't be late," she said.

I strolled out to the patio, hoping to engineer an opportunity to exchange at least a few words with Natalie. She was chatting with Vin. His profile reminded me uncomfortably of a bird of prey. When he became aware of my approach he turned his head, and I felt a tremor of disquiet as his flat, reptilian gaze assessed me. His greeting was sardonic. "It's the lady who speaks many languages."

I knew very well that Natalie, too, spoke several languages with enviable fluency, but she said, "God, I'm envious. I can usually make myself understood in Spanish, but my Portuguese is less than adequate."

Vin's face warmed as he turned back to her. "You sell

yourself short, my dear Natalie. Remember, I was with you in Brazil, and you did very well."

"Anyone for a game of billiards?" asked Innis, sauntering up with his hands still in his pockets. He'd draped a light sweater over his shoulders, and looked ready for a fashion magazine photoshoot.

"Later, perhaps," said Natalie.

She could play billiards? My opinion of her, already approaching stratospheric, went up another notch.

"Don't look at me, Innis. I'm hopeless," I declared. "That green baize stuff on the table would have furrows from one end to the other if you put a cue in my hand."

"Definitely no cues for you," said Innis. "Vin?"

"People!" Jason was all but bouncing with bonhomie as he approached us. "There's no point just standing around. What's everyone going to do with themselves this afternoon?"

"I'm trying to tempt Vin with billiards," said Innis.

"Inside on a day like this?" Jason clicked his tongue. "What a waste, when there's a swimming pool just waiting for us."

"I don't swim," said Vin, "at least, not for pleasure."

Looking at his dour expression, I wondered just what Vin *did* do for relaxation. Probably awful things to small, furry animals. "What do you do for pleasure?" I asked.

He seemed to be considering whether or not to answer my question. Then he said, "Cryptology."

"Codes, and all that stuff?"

A cold smile. "All that stuff, Diana."

He gave a subtle emphasis to my name I didn't like. It gave me the unsettling impression he was laughing at me. But why? Certainly I wasn't projecting the impression that I was the brightest bulb on the block, so maybe he was merely showing amused contempt. Or perhaps he was the undercover agent I was so sure was in place somewhere in SHO, and he was entertained by my efforts to play my role.

Jason was growing impatient. "Isn't anyone going to swim?" he asked plaintively.

"The water looked lovely," said Natalie. Her glance swept casually over me. "I think I'll take a dip."

"Great idea!" Jason was, I thought uncharitably, super keen to parade his wares again in his brief blue cozzie. "Diana? How about you?"

"Sounds good."

In the change room I found the black two-piece had dried, so I was spared the discomfort of putting on a wet costume. I'd hoped that Natalie would have to borrow one too, so I could have a chance to talk with her, but she disappeared into her guest house. I noted, for future reference, it was the one beside Innis's.

Jason, Natalie and I were the only ones interested in the water. Tecla had gone to consult with Carmina about dinner, Innis had taken Vin off for a game of billiards, and Gail had disappeared upstairs. I'd given her the mascara wand and asked her to please leave it in my room. At this very moment, I thought, Gail might well be searching my things for further incriminating items.

That thought gave me a qualm about the ersatz credit cards in my wallet, but they'd passed Carmina's examination, so I probably shouldn't worry about Gail, who'd struck me as lackluster in the brains department.

Never underestimate, a disapproving ASIO voice whispered in my head. It was a cliché to say that looks could be deceiving, but my career was living proof the statement was true. I made a silent vow to keep an eye on Gail Jones, just in case.

As the first one changed, for a few moments I had the pool to myself. I sat on the edge, dangling my feet in the aquamarine water. The afternoon sun beat gently on my shoulders. A soft breeze rustled the palms. It was so unexpectedly quiet, I fantasized that outside the garden walls there was no huge, bustling city with millions of vehicles busily criss-crossing its vast metropolitan area. Instead I imagined rolling, green hills, dotted here and there with picturesque sheep and cows. But of course green was wrong — notwithstanding the lush lawns, maintained by sprinklers, this was a harsh, semi-desert region. And the animals would be squirrels, coyotes, mountain lions, black bears. I frowned over my sparse knowledge of Southern Californian fauna. What else? Rattlesnakes?

Jason broke into my reverie. "I can tell Vin likes you," he announced, sitting down beside me. From his tone, Vin's approval was a favor greatly to be desired.

"He does?" I said doubtfully.

My disbelief brought a chuckle from Jason. "I can see why you might not think so, but I'm sure you'll find I'm right."

"You must know him well." I made it a throw-away comment. Showing too much interest in other people could be hazardous to my health. Even so, I was casting about for ways to get Jason to give me more information, as he treated Vin as a person of significance. I needed to know why.

Jason's self-regard was such he had to boast. "I do know him well. Of course" — he paused to give me a meaningful look — "it's who Vin *knows*, that makes it interesting."

Trying for a facial expression that was a tricky blend of admiration for Jason and naïve curiosity, I said, "Really? A name I'd recognize?"

"Well, you'd know, and not know him." Jason was obviously delighted to be the keeper of this individual's identity. "I can't say more," he said with false regret. "Security."

Red Wolf? I thought.

Next to me, Jason made an appreciative sound. I followed his gaze and saw Natalie. There was no way I'd ever have forgotten how stunning Siobhan — now Natalie — was, but I'd never seen her in a swimming costume before.

"Sensational," said Jason, probably feeling the same pulse of desire as I did.

Natalie, laughing, slid off the side of the pool into the water. "I'm impervious to flattery," she said.

I joined her, resigned to aimlessly splashing around until chance gave me an opportunity to have a private conversation, but was delighted to see that Jason intended to impress us with a dive from the springboard.

We formed an admiring audience of two, floating side by side, our eyes fixed on Jason as he strode down to the other end of the pool.

Without looking at me, Natalie said, "I had no idea you'd be here."

"Ditto."

She waved encouragement to Jason, who was now gently bobbing up and down on the end of the springboard. "I'm here for Red Wolf. You?"

Jason's entry into the water was untidy, but marginally better than his effort before lunch.

"What a coincidence," I said. "Me, too."

CHAPTER NINE

"Try on anything you like," said Tecla, waving me toward a room-sized walk-in wardrobe. Ostensibly I was here to take Tecla up on her offer to provide a top to go with my black skirt for this evening's dinner party, but I had a hidden agenda — to reconnoiter. I strongly suspected that Tecla had a hidden agenda, too, and not one I would welcome.

I didn't immediately enter the walk-in, but surveyed the master suite with genuine admiration. "This is just beautiful." I said, stepping forward to see more. There was no way to know if anything I learned here would be of use, but that was always the nature of undercover work — absorb as much as possible about as many things as possible.

Pleased, Tecla gestured for me to look around, saying, "I'm so glad you like it, Diana. It's my refuge, my nest." I could imagine myself here. The color scheme was principally cream and gold. The pale carpet was practically ankle-deep, the furniture had the elegance of simplicity. The bed was so large that king-size didn't describe it. Potentate-size, perhaps. The heavy bedspread added warmer color and texture to the décor, having an intricate being gold pattern on a rose-red background. There were two books on one of the bedside tables, *L'Effroyable Imposture*, and *Bin Laden: La Verite Interdite*. Judging from the feminine reading glasses, they were on Tecla's side.

"You read French?" I asked.

She'd been watching me with a faint smile. "I do. I've spent some time in France. Such a romantic language, don't you think?"

Translated, the titles were *The Horrifying Fraud* and *Bin Laden: The Forbidden Truth*. Both had been best-sellers in France, and put forward incredible scenarios. The first maintained that conspirators inside the United States government had used remote control to crash airliners into the twin towers in New York and the Pentagon in Washington. The second title explained how oil, not terrorism, was at the bottom of the war on terrorism, so the attacks on the World Trade Center were really in retaliation for the failure of secret Bush Administration negotiations over an oil pipeline slated to run through Afghanistan.

"A romantic language, but not a very romantic topic," I said.

"Have you read them? They're *so* convincing."

I'd seen the equivalent of a study guide on each, so was quite conversant with each bizarre hypothesis. "I've heard about them," I said, "that's all."

Fearing Tecla might leap on a metaphorical soapbox and start expounding on these lunatic theories, I hastened to admire a huge bay window, whose sumptuously cushioned windowseat formed an alcove where one could sit and read, or watch trees rippled by the wind.

Adjacent to the main bedroom were his-and-her bathrooms and walk-in wardrobes. "Have a look at my bathroom," said Tecla. "I think you'll like it."

Centrally featured was the sunken bath Innis had mentioned. It was larger than I'd expected, and was lined with patterned tiles. The ceiling above it was a mirror. "We have a lot of fun, here," murmured Tecla.

"I'm sure you do," I said brightly. Tecla followed me as I escaped into Jason's walk-in wardrobe. "An unusual place for a gun collection," I remarked.

A large, glass-faced cabinet displayed an arsenal of weapons — shotguns, various caliber rifles, handguns. The lower shelves were full of boxes holding a selection of different ammunition.

Tecla rested a hand lightly on my arm. "You're interested in guns?" she purred.

"Only as tools to get things done." I indicated the display. "These, though, are beautiful in their own right."

Tecla's fingers tightened on my arm. I had a feeling she was about to say something I wouldn't want to hear. I said hastily, "It's so nice of you to offer me a top. If I could just have a quick look . . ."

Her walk-in seemed to hold enough clothing to outfit a small store. "Gosh," I said, "I don't know where to start."

"This is what I'm wearing," said Tecla, indicated a simple cream dress with narrow straps. "It's a Wendy Harrison." She held it up to herself and turned towards the mirrored wall. "What do you think?"

I found I was the only one regarding our images in the mirror. Tecla was looking at me. With some alarm I noted her expression could only be described as predatory, so I skittered away to peer hopefully at a rack of clothes.

Tecla discarded her dress and strode over to a rack. "Here," she said, taking out a heavy silk tunic of cobalt blue, "try this." She delved further and came up with a black and gold top that screamed money. "Vera Wang. Don't like all her clothes, but this one's special."

Within five minutes I had six tops to try on. Tecla lingered, clearly having no intention of leaving me to my own devices. As I slipped the Vera Wang over my head, she said, "I'm so glad you like our room. Jason and I have some interesting times . . ." Her voice trailed off suggestively.

"Reading to each other in the bay window?"

She blinked, then laughed. "Not exactly."

We both surveyed my reflection in black and gold. "I don't think so," said Tecla. "Try the blue."

It was the one. The cool cobalt silk complemented my blonde hair and gave color to my nondescript greenish-brown eyes. "I don't need to try anything else. This is perfect," I said.

Although I didn't need assistance, she helped me take off the top, then put it on its padded hanger. When she handed it over I said with suitable gratitude, "Thank you so much, Tecla."

"May I be direct?"

I grinned at her. "If you must, but I know what you're going to say."

She seemed surprised. "You do?"

"I'll pay for any dry-cleaning."

"You'll *what*?"

"If I fling food down the front, I'll pay for the dry-cleaning. It's the least I can do."

Tecla shook her head. "Either you're quite extraordinary, Diana, or totally naïve. Which is it, I wonder?" When I remained silent, she went on, "Jason and I occasionally select someone special to join us."

"A threesome, you mean?"

Tecla gave a delighted smile. "Yes. Exactly."

"I'm sorry," I said, "I don't do threesomes."

"No? You're not willing to try something a little different? A walk on the wild side?"

"I'm afraid not." I took a step toward the door, but Tecla barred the way.

"Why not try it out? You'll find it . . . very erotic, very exciting." Her voice was becoming increasingly husky. "Diana, trust me. You won't be sorry."

Punctual to a fault, I was downstairs at seven o'clock. No one else had taken Tecla's admonition to heart, as apart from Jason behind the bar, I was the only person there. The entertaining area could accommodate a multitude, so even if we'd all been present — Jason, Tecla, Innis, Gail, Vin, Natalie and me — we'd only fill up one of the many islands of lounge chairs and couches designed for groups to sit and talk.

"You're first," said Jason, stating the obvious. He was leaning with spread hands on the bar, which looked as though it had been lifted whole from some upscale watering hole. Mirrored shelves behind him were lined with brightly-labeled bottles. A quick glance over the counter showed a tub of crushed ice, a glass-washing machine and a bank of refrigerated cabinets. On my side a row of bar stools awaited customers. Ashtrays, apparently purloined from British pubs, were placed at intervals along the counter. The one closest to me was emblazoned with *The Lion and Lamb*, and depicted a somnolent lion ignoring a dopey-looking lamb nestled between his front paws.

Carmina came in with Gail, both carrying bowls of mixed nuts. Carmina was dressed as the movie version of a maid, with a black dress and starchy white apron. Gail was still wearing the slacks and loose top she'd had on all day.

As Carmina placed the bowls of nuts precisely along the counter, alternating with the ashtrays, Jason said to her, "Everything in the kitchen A-OK?"

Her mouth quirked with irritation. "Of course."

"Gail?"

Gail lifted her shoulders in a shrug. "It's fine, Jason."

Watching them exit, Jason confided, "I practically drive Carmina mad, you know, but every time we have a dinner party I can't help asking if things are okay. It's the perfectionist in me." His satisfied smile indicated he considered this yet another of his excellent qualities.

"So you're super fussy?"

Jason forehead creased. "Fussy? That's not the word I'd use. Meticulous, perhaps." Belatedly remembering his duties, he asked, "Cocktail?"

Disappointed when I asked for something non-alcoholic, he said, "Oh, come on, Diana! At least champagne?"

Seeing it was Crystal, I immediately acquiesced. It was a vintage champagne I'd had once before, and never forgotten.

"That blue looks terrific on you," Jason said, passing me a fizzing glass.

"Thank you." I took a sip. It was as delicious as I remembered.

Jason tried out his rakish grin on me. Dropping his voice to an intimate half-whisper, he said, "This afternoon Tecla was going to make you an offer we hoped you couldn't refuse."

"I refused."

His grin evaporated. "She didn't tell me." He cocked his head, considering me. "You're not adventuresome?"

"Conventional to the toenails."

He leaned closer. "It doesn't have to be the three of us, you know, Diana." He let his voice slide to a sexy murmur. "It could be two, just you and me."

"Funny," I said, "that's precisely what Tecla offered."

His face darkened. "Did she?"

"I said no. It's a complication I don't need."

"What complication is that?" asked Innis, suave in a white tuxedo. He slid onto the bar stool beside me. "Well? Perhaps I can solve it for you."

Jason gave a slight shake to his head, a signal I wasn't to blurt out details of the offer I hadn't been expected to refuse.

"Identity change," I said. "Answering to a new name, and everything that goes with being a different person. When I was supposed to be Jenny Philips, I still thought of myself as Diana Loring. And now, of course, I'm here to get yet *another* identity." I sighed. "It's all a bit tiresome, really."

"Not so tiresome as being arrested for terrorism," Innis observed.

I saluted him with my glass. "Agreed! That would be *extraordinarily* tiresome."

Over his shoulder I saw Natalie entering with Vin and another man I'd not met. She was wearing something orange, a color I wouldn't have guessed would suit her, but it did. Vin was saturnine in a black suit, black shirt and — surprise — black tie. The other man was about Red Wolf's height and build, but older.

Using the artists' impressions taken from my description, ASIO had experimented with disguises that Red Wolf might assume, although there was no evidence he'd ever bothered with plastic surgery, or even grown facial hair, his anonymity being a disguise in itself. I watched the strange man move. I'd seen Red Wolf walk, although I noted nothing so distinctive as a limp, and at the time he'd been buffeted by wind and rain. There'd been a certain upright deliberateness about his gait. This man's walk was closer to a strut.

Innis, noting the direction of my gaze, swiveled around on his bar stool to say, "That's Edward Hydesmith. *Very* rich, and devoted to our cause."

"Gregory, the limo driver who picked me up at LAX, works for him."

"That's right. Edward owns a fleet of limousines, among other business ventures." He jerked his head at Tecla, who'd just appeared. "He's also devoted to my sister." A hint of malice in his smile, he added, "I'd advise you to like him, or risk Tecla's wrath — and you wouldn't want to do that."

Seeing Tecla steering Hydesmith our way, I summoned up my best welcoming face. She beamed at me, her earlier chagrin at my refusal to form a threesome apparently forgotten. "Diana," she said, "you must meet Edward."

I held out my hand to shake his, but he took the tips of my fingers and squeezed them. Yerks! I battled the impulse to snatch my hand away. Probably in his fifties, Edward Hydesmith was exquisitely groomed, as though he'd been sprayed with some agent that made his sleek white hair, his smooth tanned skin, and his practiced manner combine into one seamless, slick persona. Had she been there, Cheri would have immediately identified the particular face work he'd had. I absolutely hated him on sight.

"So you're Diana," he said. His voice had a metallic tinge and his smile didn't reach his eyes.

I agreed I was. Fortunately, further small talk at this point became unnecessary, as another guest arrived, and attention focused on him. Even Gail materialized, and made a beeline for this newcomer. She'd changed into a mud-gray outfit that was worse than unflattering. She also put her shoulder-length hair up, although stray strands were escaping.

"Who's that guy?" I asked Innis, although I knew, having read a detailed report on the man.

"Nat Upwood," said Innis, his eyes fixed on the new arrival. "He's one of our celebrity recruits, a director/writer who was really going places in the Biz, that is, until he snorted one line too many of cocaine. He's clean now, and on the comeback trail."

Innis was being kind about Nathan Upwood's history. He was talented, yes, but also a brute, who'd narrowly missed indictment for kidnapping and rape when he'd abducted and abused the supporting female lead in his wannabe-Oliver-Stone conspiracy movie, *Zero Day Down Four*, which he'd shot on a shoestring.

A plea of guilty for cocaine possession, plus a considerable payoff to the battered actress to persuade her to agree it'd been rough, but consensual sex, had led to a minimum jail sentence. Whilst in custody, Nathan Upward had followed a fine and cynical tradition, claiming to find God and emerging Born Again.

I watched Upwood as he circulated, a sullen scowl on his face. He was exactly like his photographs, a skinny, hollow-chested guy with thin brown hair and a straggly mustache that looked so fake it probably wasn't. I found it hard to imagine he had talent for anything creative, but his first two movies had gained critical, if not financial, success.

"What attracted him to SHO?" I asked Innis.

"Have you seen Upwood's films? *Zero Day Down Four* encapsulates it all." Innis had a note close to veneration in his tone. "He lays it out for anyone who has eyes to see — the World Government stooges who infest our congress and senate . . ."

I nodded, feigning interest in what he was saying, but I'd tuned Innis out so I could concentrate on a dialogue that had started behind me between Natalie and Jason. There was a buzz of conversation around us, but Natalie's cool voice was clear. She was saying, "Vin tells me there's a bomb shelter under one of the guest houses."

"That's right," said Jason, "Innis's is over it."

"A bomb shelter?" said Natalie. "I can't believe it. It's out of another era."

Jason sounded delighted to be an authority on the matter. "Wonderful example of cold war paranoia," he declared. "This house dates from the nineteen-forties, although of course it's been much improved since then. During the fifties the owner, a guy who made a fortune making plastic place mats, had a atomic bomb shelter constructed to protect his family in the event of nuclear war."

"How fascinating," said Natalie.

I was thinking how I could listen to that astringent English voice all day (and night) when she continued, "Can you still get into it?"

"We use part of it as a wine cellar."

"I'd love to have a look."

85

"Perhaps that can be arranged."

A gong sounded. "Dinner is served," Carmina announced. We went into dinner ceremonially, as dictated by Tecla. She led the procession with Hydesmith, followed by Natalie with the odious Nat Upwood, Vin and me, and Innis gallantly escorting Gail. Jason brought up the rear.

Tecla placed herself at the head of the table, with Jason at the other end. I was instructed to sit in the middle of one side, with Vin on my right hand and Edward Hydesmith on my left. Nat Upwood, Natalie, Innis and Gail shared the opposite side.

I made a few cheerfully inconsequential remarks to both Vin and Hydesmith, pushing down my visceral reaction that both were a considerable danger to me. Vin struck me as deadly as a snake, but only Hydesmith made my skin crawl.

As the dinner proceeded it became apparent Gail had a double duty: she was required to help Carmina serve the courses, but she was also a member of our company. Personally, I would have found this a trial, but Gail seemed quite content to leap up whenever Tecla signaled.

The appetizer was set before us. "Before you is shrimp in julienned green papaya with lime dressing," Tecla declared. "Asian fusion cuisine, where the best of California meets the best of Asia. It's rather an experiment Carmina and I have made, but we do hope you'll enjoy our efforts." She frowned down the table. "Jason, the wine!"

"In Australia what you call shrimp, we call prawns," I confided to Vin.

"Really?" he said without interest, his attention directed across the table to Natalie's conversation with Nat Upwood.

". . . camera would love your bone structure," Upwood was saying as he inspected Natalie's cleavage.

"Nat will be offering you a part in his next movie, next," said Innis, leaning forward to join in. He sounded envious.

"I don't believe Natalie can afford the exposure," remarked Tecla with a cool smile. She motioned for Gail to clear the plates.

While the next course, seared salmon filet with a ratatouille of tomatoes and eggplant, topped with a Thai curry sauce, was being served, I ventured a conversational aside to Hydesmith. "I just love the Beverly Hills area," I gushed. "Do you live nearby?"

This was rather a more blatant approach than I'd usually take in the circumstances. I was feeling irritable, having failed to have more than a few snatched words with Natalie, when I burned with urgent questions for her that needed fast answers.

Hydesmith was curt. "I'm in the neighborhood."

Close up, his smooth white hair didn't look quite real. I was betting a good hairpiece covered his balding scalp. I would have asked another ingenuous question, but Hydesmith's interest was clearly with what Nat Upwood was asserting with righteous passion.

"My next project will blow the lid off the training of terrorists inside the United States. I'm talking Fort Benning in Georgia."

Beside him, Natalie said, "Fort Benning? Isn't that the place that used to be called the School of the Americas?"

"The School of the Americas," Upwood repeated with corrosive scorn. "Sounds so innocent, doesn't it? But that establishment is the world's leading terrorist university. Over fifty thousand Latin Americans have graduated and then been sent home to their countries to become torturers and terrorists. That's unconscionable enough, but now the classes are being extended to American citizens, who are being trained to weaken, and ultimately destroy, the constitutionally guaranteed freedoms of the United States. The working title of my movie? *Corruption Is My Name.*"

There was a buzz of comment around the table. Jason raised his voice to say, "We need people like you in the public eye, courageous enough to speak out. The United Nations and our own immoral government condemn the very skills being taught at Fort Benning — torture, blackmail, summary execu-

87

tion, wholesale slaughter of minorities, the harassment and arrest of opponent's relatives, and so on. What hypocrites they are!"

It was almost amusing to hear the indignation in Jason's voice, considering how SHO offered safe harbor to individuals whose energies were directed toward accomplishing many of the activities he was so vehemently condemning.

"I'm sure those running Fort Benning would claim that the ends justify the means," remarked Innis.

Upwood's sallow face had become quite flushed. "Nothing justifies undermining the independence of the United States, and our individual freedoms. If people have to die for liberty, then that's the price that must be paid."

"Would you be willing to die yourself?" I asked, thinking how ironic it was that I was echoing Lawrence O'Donnell's question to me.

"Of course," Upwood snapped. "Every American at this table would."

This didn't seem likely to me. Jason was surely far too self-admiring to sacrifice himself. Gail might follow where Tecla led, but I couldn't see Tecla as a willing martyr under any circumstances. I didn't know enough about Edward Hydesmith to judge if he would relinquish his life, but I was guessing not. As for Nat Upwood, I was cynically sure he'd be disinclined to deprive Hollywood of his movie-making skills.

Dessert arrived, each plate containing a deliciously fat cream puff with spiced filling, sitting on a bed of chopped fruit. I'd been careful to drink very little during dinner, but when Jason came around with a bottle of sweet dessert wine, I succumbed. It should have been cloying, but the syrupy taste complemented the piquant tang of the cream puff's contents.

Tecla said, "Diana, Natalie, how about Rodeo Drive tomorrow, with lunch at the Regent Beverly Wilshire on me? It'll be your last chance."

"Last chance?" said Natalie. "Why? What's happening to Rodeo Drive?"

"Nothing," said Tecla, "but we're expecting a very special guest, and although you won't meet him, while he's here I'm afraid we're asking everyone to accept a security lockdown."

CHAPTER TEN

Her mouth was sweeter than any dessert wine, and far more intoxicating. We broke apart, reluctantly. "Siobhan —"

"Natalie."

"I'm sorry. That was stupid of me. Natalie." I smiled. "It quite suits you."

All day I'd been careful not to stare, to merely treat her as another guest in whom I had little interest. Now I could indulge myself, and gaze at her directly. "You look terrific," I whispered, running a finger along the line of her jaw.

Natalie smiled. "You're blonder. I like it."

I wanted to hear everything that had happened to her in all the time since we'd last met, but we didn't have the luxury of reminiscing. We were in the bathroom of her guest house, the noise of running shower in the recess beside us covering our words in case the place was wired.

It wouldn't be long before someone wondered where I was. After dinner, coffee had been served in the media center where we were to enjoy a private screening of out-takes from Upwood's *Day Zero Down Four*. The movie maker didn't hide his disgust when Natalie announced she was terribly tired and hoped he'd forgive her, but she was going to bed. I'd waited until the screening was well under way, with Upwood explaining in thorough detail every nuance of the movie's editing process, then whispered to Gail, "Is there a restroom on this floor?" and slipped out of the darkened mini-theater.

The only person I'd seen once I left the room was Gregory, the over-muscled, over-hirsute driver who'd picked me up at the airport. He was in his chauffeur's uniform, so I presumed he'd driven Hydesmith tonight. He'd looked at me as if he were about to speak, but I'd said a vague "Hi," in his direction and hurried past him in the hallway.

I knew I was taking a significant chance, but I had to learn what Natalie was doing here, and what she knew. Taking both her hands in mine, I leaned into her so my mouth was close to her ear. Speaking just loud enough to be heard above the splashing water, I said, "Our intelligence says Red Wolf will make a simultaneous attack on the Diablo Canyon and San Onofre nuclear reactors. Is that what you've heard?"

"I'm almost sure that's a red herring, if you'll forgive the pun."

"What, then?"

"I don't know. I tried obliquely to find out from Vin, but I couldn't push it too hard."

"Vin — who is he?"

We sat on the edge of the bath, our heads close together. Natalie said, "The man's changed identities so often I doubt we could ever find who he really is, but Vincent de Costa is the name he's using now. None of that matters, though, it's who Vin represents."

"Red Wolf."

She nodded. "Vin's his right hand man. Think of him as a combined manager and booking agent. Vin smoothes the way for him, makes all the arrangements. After everything checks out, Vin gives the okay, and Red Wolf comes in."

I asked how she'd met up with this key player in Red Wolf's organization.

"I've impeccable credentials through Edification," she breathed against my cheek, "and had no trouble arranging a meeting in Buenos Aires, once the promise of a great deal of money for future services rendered was made. We traveled to various places in South America. The details don't matter now, the important thing is that Vin trusts me, at least as much as he's likely to trust anyone."

Natalie, real name Mary Siobhan Hurdstone, worked for the privately-funded Hurdstone Peace Foundation established by her philanthropic father with the goal of promoting peace and fighting terrorism. She had been undercover for several years in Edification, an international terrorist organization, where I'd met her while on assignment. It had been thought at the time that ASIO's efforts had broken Edification's back, but this assessment proved far too optimistic. Siobhan/Natalie had remained undercover in the organization to monitor developments.

I checked my watch. Time was passing and there was still so much to learn. "How do you know the Skinners?"

"Initially, we were after Red Wolf. We had reliable intelligence that his representative in negotiations was Vin de Costa, so I traveled to South America to meet him."

I shook my head in admiration. "Bloody hell, that's more than the combined might of Western intelligence agencies could discover."

It wasn't the first time the Hurdstone Peace Foundation had embarrassed various governments with superior intelligence information. I could imagine Lawrence O'Donnell's angry reaction when he found out about this latest coup.

"Private enterprise," said Natalie with a grin, "you can't beat it."

She explained while she'd been in Buenos Aires, the Foundation had contacted her with the information about the Skinners' involvement in a future strike in Los Angeles by Red Wolf. Fortunately Edification, as part of its efforts to establish new links worldwide, had already contacted SHO some months before, so when Natalie told Vin de Costa that she'd be traveling to California to meet up with the Skinners, his initial suspicions were quickly allayed.

"Vin's a dangerous man," Natalie said. "I get on with him as well as anybody, but I always remind myself he could turn on me in an instant."

I had the same misgivings, but discussing Vin's potential deadliness wouldn't advance my knowledge of the present situation. "Red Wolf," I said. "What's your plan of action?"

"I'm not here to take him out. He's too hard a target, although if the opportunity presented itself I'd go for it."

"What, then?"

Her smile made my heart turn over. "The plan's to become Vin's second-best friend, and learn as much as possible about the structure and running of the organization. It'd be a bonus if I got a glimpse of Red Wolf's face. Of course, if I achieved that, I'd have to find a reason to get out, fast."

She nuzzled my neck. "Your turn."

"I've seen his face. Red Wolf's."

She drew back to look at me. "Does he know that you've seen him?"

"Yes, although it's possible he believes I'm dead."

"My God," said Natalie.

I knew what she was thinking. If Vin or the Skinners discovered I could identify Red Wolf, my life expectancy would be close to zero. No, it would be less than zero.

* * * * *

"Oh, here you are," said Tecla, her tone sharp. She stood over me, a drink and cigarette in one hand, the other on her hip. She'd kicked off her stiletto heels and was barefoot.

I was stretched out on a poolside lounge, hands behind my head. The underwater lighting provided the only illumination, but I could see her distrustful expression quite clearly.

I sat up, saying, "Tecla, please forgive me. I know I should appreciate Nat Upwood's movie, but I don't, and all those out-takes and his endless explanations bored me to tears. So I made an excuse to sneak out. I hoped he wouldn't notice. Did he?"

"Probably not, but I did."

Her taut body language was loosening a little, so I went on, "It was rude of me, I admit, but it would have been ruder still if I'd dosed off in the middle of it all, don't you think?"

Slightly mollified, Tecla conceded this point. "So where have you been? What have you been doing with yourself?"

"Do you want me to be totally truthful?"

Tecla took a hard draw on her cigarette. "Of course. I wouldn't advise you to lie to me — ever."

"Have you been to the Philippines? Or Indonesia? Not the cities. I mean, out in the country, in the villages, where life's a struggle."

After setting her glass on a table, Tecla sat down on the lounge next to mine. "It's not a part of the world I've visited."

Summoning up my best creative abilities, I said, "I've spent almost two years in South East Asia, always on the run, moving from place to place, often dealing with people I feared might slit my throat while I slept. I don't mean I've lost my convictions because of what I've been through, but you can't imagine how nice is to be here, safe, in a beautiful house in one of the great cities of the world." I gestured at the glowing blue of the pool. "And, Tecla, to have clean water, not some fetid pond full of mosquito larvae . . ."

That's enough. Don't overdo it, Denise.

Tecla's mouth had relaxed. "I think I can understand

94

that." She leaned over to stub out her cigarette in the nearest ashtray.

"So I've been out here luxuriating. Watching the lights of aircraft way up overhead, listening to the night sounds, just letting everything soak in."

Either I'd won Tecla over, or she was a master at deception. "I absolutely understand," she said, her voice soft. She stood, taking my hand as she did so, and pulling me to my feet. Without her shoes on, I was a good half-head taller.

Looking up at me, she said, "We've got a busy day shopping tomorrow. I think you should go to bed."

When I looked at her sideways, she chuckled. "Your own bed, alone," she said, "at least for tonight . . ."

CHAPTER ELEVEN

No self-respecting establishment in Beverly Hills opened before ten, so on Saturday morning there was no hurry to get underway on our shopping excursion. I hid my impatience. The Skinners' house was being watched, all the comings and goings monitored closely, so Ben Attwood would know when I left the premises and where I went. Wandering around boutiques and department stores would present perfect opportunities to exchange information. I was sure he'd take advantage of that.

Lying awake last night, I'd debated whether to put what I'd learned in written form, with the hope of passing a note to an agent shadowing our progress from one luxury shop to another. I'd decided against it, believing Tecla or Jason quite capable of strip-searching me on a whim. Besides, something as concrete as a note could be seen, and maybe retrieved. Spoken words, in contrast, dissolved into thin air.

Presiding over a late breakfast, Tecla declared, "Diana, I don't want you to use those credit cards you've got. They'd be too easy to trace. If you're only window-shopping, fine, but if you do buy anything, I'll put it on my Amex card. You can pay me back later, in cash."

Jason wasn't at the table, but Natalie and Vin were seated together. Before I'd parted from Natalie last night, I'd asked, "Just what does being second-best friends with Vin involve? Going to bed with him?"

She'd made a face and said she devoutly hoped not. Now, seeing them together, I felt a pang of envy — I didn't want to call it jealousy — as Vin casually touched her shoulder.

"Behold the ladies preparing to descend on Rodeo Drive," said Innis, entering the room with his usual saunter. "How very Beverly Hills that is."

"You spend half your life buying clothes there," his sister retorted, "so don't criticize us."

Innis made a face at her. "So what's so great about all those elegant boutiques selling prestigious labels at very high prices? Have you told our guests they'll be battling hoards of tourists?" With a sardonic smile, he added, "And every last tourist will be scanning for the rich and famous."

Shopping as a pastime had never particularly interested me. I'd never understood how browsing with nothing particular in mind entertained so many people. I followed the Denise Cleever rule of painless shopping: know what you want, find it, purchase it, leave. Therefore, under other circumstances, I would have been distinctly underwhelmed at the prospect of spending hours in department stores and shops, however exclusive they might be. Today, of course, was an exception.

When I checked what of my meager wardrobe I should wear for such an excursion, Tecla said, "I don't know whether it's the tourists, or the influence of Hollywood, but you can wear anything you like in Beverly Hills these days, from jeans right through to high fashion." She added, her disapproval plain, "Standards have gone to hell in a handbasket."

I took her at her word, and came downstairs just after ten wearing my best jeans and a handprinted top from the Philippines, which was actually quite beautiful. No one else was ready, so I had to while away the time talking to Innis, who was still at the dining room table, drinking coffee and making his leisurely way through the fat Saturday edition of the *L.A. Times.* "Did you see this?" he said, indicating a headline on the front page, SECURITY ALERT AT ATOMIC PLANTS. "What do you think?"

I shrugged. "Aren't there security alerts all the time, and nothing happens?"

"Something will happen, sooner or later." He gave me a lazy grin. "And I'd put my money on sooner, rather than later."

Feigning a faint alarm, I said, "Jeez, we're not too close to one of those atomic plants, are we?"

"Relax, Diana, you're perfectly safe from *radiation.*" He had the pleased manner of someone who had superior knowledge of something important. "You can rely on that."

"So I'm not going to be irradiated. That's a comfort. But do I have to worry about something else?"

Innis shook his head, smiling. "I can't say."

Punching his arm gently, I said, "Oh, go on, tell me." I added with a touch of doubt, "If you really know, that is."

He put his finger to his lips. "Tecla would kill me."

"Tecla would kill you for what?" Jason said from the doorway. This morning he was wearing brief white shorts and a tight blue T-shirt. He gave me the benefit of a cosmetic dentist's work. "What's he been telling you, Diana?"

"His take on today's headlines."

Still grinning, Jason came over and roughly ruffled Innis's hair. He laughed aloud when his brother-in-law batted at him, furious. "None of us takes Innis all that seriously," he said.

Innis didn't reply, but if looks could kill, Jason would have turned up his toes, then and there.

It was nearly eleven when Natalie and I piled into Tecla's Jaguar for the short drive to Wilshire Boulevard, where the upmarket department stores of Neiman Marcus, Saks Fifth Avenue and Barneys New York sat on adjacent blocks. Rodeo Drive, Tecla had decided, could wait for after lunch, when we'd be fortified for serious shopping.

We sat in the drive while Tecla blew the Jag's horn in a series of staccato blasts. Gail came rushing out of the house. "Sorry!" she exclaimed, bundling herself into the car.

I wondered why Gail was accompanying us, but once we were in Neiman Marcus her role became evident. Gail had been instructed to become my shadow. When Tecla and Natalie wandered away in different directions, Gail hovered close beside me. When I drifted toward the shoes, she came too. When I lingered at the chocolate counter — so tempting — Gail lingered too.

A niggling worry persisted. Did the Skinners have suspicions about me? Perhaps I hadn't really convinced Tecla last night. Why wasn't Natalie getting the same treatment? But then, she'd been validated by her association with Vin, and her role in Edification. My history held up to examination, but I didn't have Natalie's credentials. Maybe it was simply an understandable precaution, taken because Red Wolf was about to be an honored guest.

I felt like saying to Gail, "Bloody hell! I can find my own way around a department store, so leave me alone."

If I complained, I was sure Gail would look at me with her doughy face blank. "I don't know what you're talking about," she'd say.

How could I get rid of the blasted woman? If I did anything unusual, or had a few quick words with a stranger, Gail would be there to observe, and report back to Tecla.

As a fallback position, I'd decided if no one contacted me by mid-afternoon, I'd take a gamble and slip away to find a payphone and call the emergency contact number. With Gail dogging my steps, this now seemed impossible.

Last night I'd been tempted to use the credit card phone in the garden, but I couldn't be sure the electronic monitoring Tecla had mentioned was confined to the house. There was always the vexing thought the monitoring of phone calls she described didn't exist, but the simple possibility was an effective disincentive.

I had important information to impart. Red Wolf's arrival was likely tonight or on Sunday. Vin de Costa had to be named as Red Wolf's main associate. I'd also have to explain why Natalie was there, and mention her belief the nuclear plants weren't the real targets, a fact that seemed to be confirmed indirectly by Innis this morning.

Natalie's presence in the Skinners' house was sure to cause impotent fury in Washington because of the involvement of the Hurdstone Foundation, but there was nothing to be done about it without aborting the assignment, and there was no way that would happen.

I wished I didn't have to mention Natalie at all. The more people who knew about her role, the more danger she'd be in. In a perfect world, intelligence agencies wouldn't leak classified information about individuals. In the real world, there was always some seepage.

Gail tapped me on the arm. I snarled. I've always hated being tapped. Gail pouted. "Tecla says we're walking down to Saks. Okay?"

"Okay." I joined Tecla and Natalie and we went out into a perfect day. The sky was blue, the breeze was mild, money streamed down Wilshire — Jags and Cadillacs, Mercs and Beemers, scads of luxury four-wheel drives — fetchingly called sports utility vehicles here in the States — and expensive convertibles, driven, it seemed, almost exclusively by balding, middle-aged men.

Saks and Barneys were mirror images of Neiman Marcus. All the best labels, all the most exclusive, expensive gear, all

100

employing staff who materialized with unnerving alacrity when a potential sale was scented.

By the time we set off in the direction of lunch, I was convinced Tecla was born to shop as well as to save America from World Government conspirators. Her platinum American Express card had taken a severe beating, and we had the afternoon still before us.

Gail was sent off laden with parcels and bags to collect the car and drive it the few blocks to the Regent Beverly Wilshire hotel, while Tecla, Natalie and I walked, breaking our progress with stops at a few smaller, but no less exclusive shops.

From the time we'd hit the first department store I'd been covertly scanning other shoppers, trying to identify a contact. I knew no one would approach me with Gail sticking so close. I saw a couple of possibilities; one a well-dressed, titian-haired woman who seemed to turn up in all the departments I visited in Neiman Marcus. I crossed her off when she was met by a similar Beverly Hills matron with cries of extravagant joy. After much air-kissing they'd departed for the store restaurant, which I'd noticed nestled discreetly on the lower ground floor.

In Barneys, dressed as conservatively as any agent under O'Donnell's watch, a young man had appeared promising, as he seemed to be tracking Gail and me. Eventually he checked his watch, and without a glance in my direction, went hurrying out of the store.

I couldn't imagine we would spend much time in the smaller shops that lined our route to lunch, but we did. In each one sales staff hovered, as Natalie (desultorily) and Tecla (keenly) examined merchandise. Tecla seemed to be keeping an eye on me, and when I experimentally strayed to the back of one establishment, she found it necessary to drift that way too.

Then, at last, lunch. Pretending to be interested in shopping had generated a healthy appetite. The Regent Beverly Wilshire, at the corner of Wilshire Boulevard and Rodeo

Drive, was a grand hotel in the true sense of the word. The Lobby Lounge (more relaxed, Tecla said, than the formal dining room) was beautiful, with warm paneling and floor length windows. A gigantic floral arrangement dominated the room. Agreeable background music was provided by a pianist at a grand piano.

When we arrived, we found Gail sitting in an alcove near the entrance. From her expression, she'd been waiting for some time. As we were taken to our table I glanced around, wondering if I would pick up a circumspect signal. Gail would have been tailed as she drove the Jaguar to the hotel and valet parked, and when she went to the waiting area for the Lobby, our luncheon destination would have been clear.

Under different circumstances I would have very much enjoyed Natalie's company. However, with Gail and Tecla there, the conversation was superficial chatter. The menu was not extensive, but the food proved delicious. We were onto coffee when I heard an unmistakable sniff.

Maddie Parkes was in the process of being seated at a table close by. Her sleek red hair gleamed, and a gold bracelet caught the light as she took off her dark glasses. Her companion was the young man I'd seen in Barneys New York.

The conversation at our table concerned funny and/or disastrous shopping experiences. I watched each person's face as she spoke, and laughed at the appropriate spots, but I was listening hard. Another sniff. I found it almost endearing. After the waiter had taken their orders, Maddie said, "Where's the restroom, please?"

I gave her two minutes, then excused myself and followed her. Naturally Gail exclaimed, "Wait for me, I'm coming too," as she hastily put down her coffee cup.

"I get the feeling you're shadowing me," I said as we walked down a short corridor.

Gail gave me the totally blank look I'd expected. "I don't get what you mean."

"Everywhere I've been today, you've been there too."

"Well, of course. We were shopping together."

"I'll smack you one, if you don't stop," I said, quite pleasantly.

Her jaw dropped slightly. "What?"

"You heard me. And don't think I won't."

We'd come to a paneled door with the discreet sign that indicated only ladies entered here. "You're not thinking of coming into the stall with me, are you?" I asked as I pushed it open.

She actually blushed. "Of course not!"

The restroom of the Regent Beverly Wilshire hotel was, I decided, one of the great restrooms of the world. It was quiet, luxurious, individual handtowels rolled up in tight little cylinders, the lighting flattering, so a view of oneself in one of the many mirrors did not cause anguish. More importantly, the toilet stalls were actually paneled roomettes, each made totally private by full-length walls and a heavy, polished wooden door.

There was no one else in view. As I couldn't see Maddie, she had to be behind one of the doors. Pausing, as though about to enter one, I glared at Gail. "Are you going to lurk out here like some sick pervert?"

The had the desired effect. She barged past me into a toilet stall, slamming the door behind her.

There was one larger door facing me at the end of the little corridor of stalls. It opened as soon as Gail had disappeared, and Maddie beckoned me in. This was the handicapped facility, a legal requirement in all public restrooms. The Regent Beverly Wilshire's classy version was a like a spacious private bathroom, with an elegant counter and basin at one end.

Shutting the door behind me, I said, "Is this soundproof?"

"Yes."

"We've got to be quick."

Maddie gave a throaty laugh. "Quickies turn me on."

"Oh, *please!*"

She whipped out a voice-activated recorder. "Say it fast, then."

In an urgent whisper I ripped through the points I had to make, my words running into each other. In less than two minutes I'd finished.

"That's it?" said Maddie.

"So far."

"Okay, I've got this for you. The atomic plants almost certainly are a smokescreen. We don't know specific targets, but latest intelligence is that Red Wolf's team will be using bioterrorism. Anthrax to be exact."

It was a relief to know I'd recently been vaccinated against anthrax. I said, "Our response?"

"Top level security — need to know only. To avert widespread panic, no public announcements, no mass vaccinations. Right now, millions of doses of Cipro are on the way to California, to be held in reserve in case they're needed."

"An attack timetable?"

She made a face. "It's vague. Next week some time."

Outside, Gail had to be getting suspicious. "I've got to go."

"Two things more. First, since no doubt the Skinners have already searched you, Ben believes it's now safe to give you this." It was a miniature hearing device, very like a deaf person's hearing aid.

"Second, there's been an amendment to your mission. Everything's as before, but if in your judgement, you've got an assured chance to terminate, take it."

"Or die trying?"

"Don't die," she said, and amazed me by leaning forward and kissing my cheek.

A few seconds later I was out in the main part of the washroom, drying my hands on one of the little towels, leaving Maddie behind the closed door of the handicapped bathroom.

"Why'd you take so long?" Gail demanded.

"You don't want to know," I said. I lowered my voice to a

confidential level. "It's a hereditary problem, Gail. And a bit messy."

She didn't want to go there. "Right," she said, "we'd better get back."

Rodeo Drive began and ended with residential neighborhoods. The world-famous section was only a few blocks situated right in the heart of the Beverly Hills shopping district. Innis had been right about tourists, they were everywhere, cameras and credit cards to the ready. Gail still shadowed me, but at a respectful distance. Gucci, Ferragamo, Chanel, Fendi, Tiffany, Van Cleef & Arpels, Lladro, Giorgio Armani, Versace, Dior, Cartier, Bulgari — after a while, the names blurred.

At last we were finished, had collected the car, and were on our way back to base. Back to lockdown. Red Wolf. The very real possibility of losing my life.

CHAPTER TWELVE

"I monstered Gail," I said to Tecla. "Did she tell you?"

Natalie, Tecla and I were seated out on the patio, consuming coffee and cake to rally us after the rigors of the day.

My declaration amused Tecla. "Gail did complain you threatened her with bodily harm."

Natalie looked appropriately perplexed. "What did Gail do, for heaven's sake?"

"She stalked me. Wherever I went, she went too. Didn't you notice?"

Natalie shrugged her lack of interest. "My attention was elsewhere."

"I'd do the same in your place, Tecla," I said. "Keep an eye on me, I mean."

She raised her eyebrows. "Would you?"

"Yeah. I'm the super-cautious type. That's how I got out of South East Asia in one piece."

"For someone so cautious," Tecla observed, "you managed to make it pay. Our fees are not cheap."

I sent her a conspiratorial grin. "Hey, nobody said political activism couldn't be profitable. For example, look at you." I made a sweeping gesture to encompass both Tecla and our surroundings.

Complacent with what she took as a warm compliment, Tecla said, "Money's power. The more money, the more power."

"Is that why Edward Hydesmith's investing in SHO? For power?"

My question brought a frown to Tecla's face. "Why are you so interested in Edward?"

"I was hoping to eventually persuade him to invest in overseas activism." Cheeky grin to indicate my impudence. "Like maybe in South East Asia . . ."

Tecla laughed. "You're a piece of work, Diana!"

I was modest. "Thank you."

Natalie, who'd been pensively consuming carrot cake, said to Tecla, "Didn't I hear you telling Jason that Hydesmith would be here tonight?"

"You've got sharp ears." Her tone indicated this was not a commendation.

"I've always had excellent hearing," said Natalie, taking Tecla at her word.

Tecla pursed her lips. "There are times when it's better not to see, or hear, certain things."

As she spoke, Vin came out of the house. His gaunt face purposeful, he strode across the patio to our table. He really did wear clothes well, I thought, looking at the way his linen slacks and crisp shirt hung on his lean frame.

"Tecla, I need to speak with you." His voice had an indefinable accent, giving it a foreign but not unpleasing cadence.

107

She got up immediately. "Of course."

Watching them go back into the house, Natalie said, "I believe this is one of those times we're not to see or hear certain things." She said it with a slight smile, so anyone observing would think she'd made some inconsequential remark.

Keeping a carefree expression on my face, and taking care my body language indicated I was at ease, I murmured, "I reckon a certain party's about to arrive. Did you know there's a separate apartment upstairs that can be kept isolated from the rest of the house?"

Natalie stretched and yawned. "No, I didn't."

"You can get to it from outside. There's a private entrance around the side of the house. Stairs lead directly up to the apartment. Where we are now, we couldn't see anyone going in, because there's a fence and assorted shrubs in the way."

"Then I believe we can relax and enjoy the roses."

Surrounding the patio were rose gardens of splendid profusion. When I'd commented how lovely they were, Tecla had said the climate in this part of L.A. particularly suited the growing of roses. This certainly was the case here: magnificent blooms of white, deep pink, scarlet, yellow, and pastel shades of apricot and mauve, hung heavy on the bushes.

I pointed, as though admiring a particular flower, and said, "Anthrax is a distinct possibility. I hope you're vaccinated."

Natalie contemplated her sandalled feet. "Diana, do you wear nail polish on your toenails?"

Innis spoke from behind me. "Nail polish should only be worn if one has beautiful feet. Are yours surpassingly attractive, Diana?"

"I've lately come to think they're my best feature," I declared. "How about *your* metatarsals, Innis?"

"Close to flawless." His grin faded. "Now, if you don't mind, ladies, we're all going downstairs to have a nice game of billiards."

* * * * *

I went down the stairs to the billiard room thinking of anthrax. For Red Wolf and his team to use this deadly bacteria as a weapon, the spores had to be dried, milled to a particular particle size and then effectively distributed to infect large numbers of people. I had no doubt he had access to the laboratories and personnel necessary to get supplies. Heightened public awareness, due to the earlier attack using the United States mail to deliver anthrax-laced envelopes to individuals in the media and government, meant that the mere rumor that this substance had been used once again would almost guarantee widespread alarm and panic.

Within six days, those infected with anthrax spores would develop fever, fatigue and chest pain, followed by severe breathing problems. There was one bright spot about anthrax, however. Antibiotics were successful in most cases if provided within three to seven days of exposure to the bacteria.

Gail and Carmina were waiting for us when we came down the stairs to the billiard room. Obviously the idea was to keep the four of us out of the way while Red Wolf was brought in. In one corner Carmina was perched on a chair reading a Spanish-language newspaper. Gail was pacing around, indicating she'd not taken kindly to her inclusion in the category of security risk. She kept shooting furious glances at our nonchalant jailer, who seemed oblivious to her attempts to convey her resentment.

Innis handed Natalie a cue and took one himself. It seemed he intended that we carry the charade through, and actually have a game.

"You play?" I said to Gail, jerking my head at the massive, green baize table.

Gail turned her angry gaze on me. "Not with you, I won't."

"There's no way I'm giving a cue to Diana, anyway," said

109

Innis. "Jason's finicky about the surface of this table, and Diana has already admitted she's a danger to baize in general."

"Then we'll just watch, won't we, Gail?" I said with a cheery, lets-make-the-best-of-it tone.

She rolled her eyes, sneered, then stalked over to a chair into which she flung herself. Congeniality did not appear to be high on her list of attributes to cultivate.

"Overkill, Gail," I said, clicking my tongue in disapproval. "The rolling eyes, yes. Or the sneer. Not both."

Over in the corner I saw Carmina, her head still inclined over her newspaper, smile to herself. It didn't surprise me that she might not feel goodwill toward Gail, as frankly, the woman was hard to put up with at the best of times.

Natalie and Innis began to take turns to ricochet balls around the table, and I noted with absent-minded pleasure that she seemed to be much more skilled than Innis. I propped myself against the wall, arms folded, to think about why we'd been herded down here to the basement.

It was puzzling. Why not leave us on the patio? Red Wolf's mode of transport, probably a large SUV with tinted windows, would come through the gates and up the drive to stop in front of the Skinners' home. Nothing could be seen from the street. He could get out, walk around the side of the house, open the door, go up the stairs, and there he would be, safe in his private lair.

So why move us down here?

Unless he wasn't coming in that way. But why not? The side entrance was entirely protected from the neighbor's sightline by the two-meter stone fence and a row of trees planted along the boundary. He could enter through the main door and go up the curving stairway and through the private, locked door, and into the apartment that way. Natalie and I would still not have seen him from the patio.

Unless he entered through the garden, but that was impossible. There was no back entrance to the Skinners' house, as neighbors' grounds abutted the property on three sides.

The unsettling impression I'd overlooked something was worrying me. I visualized the floor plans I'd studied. They had been very detailed, showing the grounds, fences and placement of vegetation, as well as the layout of the basement and the two floors of the house. The bomb shelter built by a previous owner in the nineteen-fifties had been marked on the plans as sealed, although I recalled Natalie's conversation with Jason yesterday evening where he'd said they used part of it as a wine cellar.

The guest house Innis occupied had been built over the site of the shelter, so presumably the entrance to the wine cellar was somewhere in his place. He'd quite freely shown his living quarters to me, so I could mentally skip from room to room, trying to find anything that would indicate an entrance to the shelter.

Perhaps it was outside, in the manner of those storm cellars that have double trap doors which open to give access to the area beneath. I'd never actually seen one of these storm cellars. They were very familiar from movies, usually being featured when families were fleeing a raging tornado, or in horror movies, when impossibly daring characters went waltzing underground, even though everything indicated something nasty was lurking there.

"What are you thinking about so earnestly?" Innis asked. It was Natalie's turn to whack balls around the table, so Innis could turn his attention my way.

"Frivolous things," I said. "What else?"

Leaning negligently on his cue, he contemplated me. Looking past him, I could see that Gail, still slumped in a chair, was listening closely.

"I like you," said Innis. Gail's face showed disgust.

He went on, "You amuse Tecla. That's quite an achievement. But don't push it too far."

"Meaning?"

"My sister's a charmer — I'd be the first to admit that. She's also totally ruthless. And frequently a liar. My advice to you is, watch out."

Again, there was that hint of self-satisfied, I'm-in-the-know.

Glancing at Gail, I saw that she was staring at Innis with an odd expression. At a guess I'd say it was half outrage he'd impugned her boss, and half grudging agreement he was right about her.

"Thank you, Innis," I said.

He cocked his head. "And just how thankful are you?"

I grinned at him. "Not quite that thankful."

"Your turn, Innis," said Natalie. "I believe I've snookered myself."

We were released half an hour later, when Jason called down to say we could come up. Gail, who'd maintained a sullen, glowering silence, skittered away up the stairs like a balloon released into a wind.

I followed more sedately, although my thoughts were bubbling. I found myself full of a weird kind of optimism. Everything had been prepared for this day when I'd be physically so close to Red Wolf that his capture became a real possibility. He'd have aides with him, bodyguards and assistants, but I was the one who could point and say, "That one. That's Red Wolf."

It was a heady feeling, but touched with a quiver of terror. Wasn't I entirely too confident I'd recognize him? Could I really be instrumental in bringing down one of the most successful terrorists in the world? A man who at this moment would have members of his network in place at targets in Los Angeles, poised to infect an unsuspecting public, grown com-

112

placent when each new warning of a terrorist attack turned out to be a false alarm.

Jason met us at the top of the stairs, his face glowing with barely suppressed elation. One lock of his dark hair fell artfully across his forehead. It was obvious Red Wolf's arrival had gone according to plan, and the fact he was safely installed in the apartment clearly gave Jason great pleasure.

So energized he was almost dancing on the spot, he exclaimed, "Diana! Natalie!" and took each of our hands, as if greeting us after a long separation.

Innis, coming up the stairway behind us, regarded all this with a sour face. "Jesus, Jason, calm down."

Jason's smile didn't falter. "There's a good day coming, Innis. A *good* day."

His pleasure was not even slightly dented, I thought, by the realization he would be an accessory to the murder of many people, killed by the use of what the politicians loved to call, with fittingly sonorous tones, "a weapon of mass destruction."

Jason released Natalie's hand, and took mine in both his. Pressing them firmly, he said, "I have a favor to ask of you, my dear Diana. I can't explain why, but I'm afraid I have to ask you to move out of your room."

"Oh, I know why," I said. "I've been snoring again, haven't I?"

Natalie gave a snort of laughter. "Such an attractive trait," she said.

Jason smiled the smile of one who's not sure if he's got the joke, but doesn't want to be thought slow on the uptake. "It's a logistic matter," he said.

I freed my fingers. "Where do you want me to go?"

He gave me a look of enthusiastic entreaty, although we both knew I really had no choice. "One of the guest houses is empty. If you don't mind . . ."

On one level, I did mind. In the main house I would be

that much closer to Red Wolf. However, in one of the little guest houses, I'd be that much closer to Natalie. "I'll just have to cope," I said.

I glanced Natalie's way, casually, a tremor of desire zipping through me.

"I hope the soundproofing's adequate," she said. "I can't abide snoring."

We had a special link, she and I. Of all people, Natalie understood from her own experience what it was like to be undercover, inhabiting an identity not your own. She had shared the exhilaration of risking your life, and surviving. Of living by your wits, with no safety net to save you. She knew the sheer terror of those moments when you skated close to exposure.

It was a life I'd come to need, like the pull of an addiction. It wasn't just the rush that came from danger conquered. There was something there, too, about my commitment to my country and the way of life Australia stood for, plus the conviction that, although members of the general public would never know it, what I was doing often made a real difference to their future lives.

I thought of others who'd touched me deeply in the past. There was always an area of my life I could never explain, not just because of the official secrets act, but because I couldn't hope to convey what it was really like to someone who had never experienced anything remotely similar.

"I'll help you move your things, if you like." Natalie sounded as if she hoped I wouldn't accept her offer.

"Oh, would you?" I said. "That'd be great."

Natalie grunted, graciousness itself. Jason's smile widened. "I'll make it up to you, Diana, really I will. In just a few days."

"I'll hold you to that."

He chortled at this, clearly reading more into my words than I intended. With a mighty effort I resisted clobbering him.

Natalie trailed up the main staircase behind me, doing a good imitation of reluctant assistance. When we gained my room I whispered, "Tonight?"

Her luscious mouth quirked. "If you insist."

Dinner was a low key affair, which Carmina served with admirable efficiency. The appetizer was salad, the main course pepper steak, mashed potatoes, creamed spinach. Wine was provided, but I noticed neither Jason nor Tecla was drinking. Innis appeared to be making up the slack, however. I sipped delicately at my Chardonnay, stretching it out. There was no way I could afford to dull the edge of my perceptions.

It was a perfectly amiable table, made doubly so by the absence of both Vin and of Edward Hydesmith. I'd expected Hydesmith at dinner, but apparently his appearance would be later in the evening. Jason had lost none of his ebullience. Tecla seemed complacently satisfied. Innis was thoughtful, although his introspection may have been brought on by the quantity of alcohol he was consuming. Even Gail wore an expression approaching affability.

Natalie chatted brightly with Jason about South America. I threw in a few bland comments, although I was rather thrown by the hearing device I was wearing. It was a tiny capsule pushed deep into the channel of my left ear. Anyone directing a beam of light into my ear would see it; however, as nobody could possibly know I had the device, I was reasonably sure I was safe.

Although I'd practiced with similar gadgets, I'd never had

occasion to wear one in the field, and found it very disconcerting to have my own words picked up by bone conduction and amplified in booming volume inside my skull.

Every time I turned my head, newly magnified sounds impinged. I was puzzled by an odd frying noise, until I realized it was the bubbles rising in Tecla's glass of mineral water.

Carmina was serving coffee and selected cheeses when Hydesmith burst into the room. "Jason, I must speak to you at once!"

Jason leapt to his feet and hurried after him. Tecla, her face concerned, rose. "Please, enjoy your coffee. I'll only be a moment."

As she left the room I positioned my head for optimum reception. I was getting better at this, because immediately I picked up the conversation in the hall outside. It was extraordinary to hear clearly through the closed door.

Hydesmith was saying, ". . . a fucking disaster!"

Jason said, "Does he suspect you know?"

"Of course not. Do I look like a fool? The question is, what do we do now?"

Tecla intervened with, "We have to deal with this ourselves. Not involve our special guest. When the matter's resolved, we can tell him."

"When will de Costa be back?" Hydesmith was sounding thoroughly rattled.

"Vin? Not until tomorrow morning." Tecla took charge, her tone sharp. "Jason, you know what to do. We've discussed this scenario a hundred times. Get what you need, go with Edward, deal with it."

A few moments later she was back in the dining room, smiling like the practiced hostess she was.

"Something wrong?" said Innis.

"A minor problem. You know how Edward blows the smallest thing into a full scale catastrophe."

He nodded, not entirely convinced.

Their urgent tones had made it sound like a truly full scale catastrophe to me. "Will Mr. Hydesmith be joining us?" I asked.

Tecla's smile disappeared. "Later, perhaps." She frowned at Innis, who was tossing back the last of the red wine in his glass. As he reached for the bottle, she snapped, "Innis!"

"What?"

She made an effort to sound lighthearted. "You don't want a fuzzy head tomorrow, brother mine."

"Don't worry about me." Catching the withering look she blasted at him, he put the bottle down. "Perhaps you're right."

Why she wanted Innis sober — or at least less drunk — was soon evident. He was again to perform the role of our keeper, although this time, neither Carmina nor Gail would be included in the party. It seemed to be a precaution only. Tecla wasn't uptight about it, merely asking if we'd mind spending the rest of the evening out of the house in the garden or the guest houses.

"Why doesn't Tecla want us inside?" I asked Innis as he, Natalie and I strolled through the cool evening air.

He halted, hands in his pockets, and rocked gently heel to toe. "Wouldn't you like to know?"

"Well, yes, I would. That's why I'm asking."

He dropped his voice to a whisper. "It's a secret."

Natalie linked her arm through his. "We're good at keeping secrets. That's what we do."

This seemed to amuse him. He made a gallant sweep with his free arm. "Come into my place. Maybe you can persuade me to tell you."

"I've already told Tecla I'm not into threesomes," I said severely.

Innis giggled. I exchanged a look with Natalie. Perhaps we could get him to talk. "Have you got anything to drink?" I asked.

"Of course."

"Then you're on, matey."

CHAPTER THIRTEEN

Innis was on his fourth Scotch. "I'm drinking too much," he observed, raising his glass and peering at it as if surprised to find it in his hand.

I raised my rum and Coke in a toast. "To the future," I said.

We all solemnly drank. Natalie had taken over the bar duties, and was keeping Innis well supplied. Like me, she had been nursing the same drink, in her case a gin and tonic, for some time.

Innis had turned his television set on as soon as we entered. Images danced across the screen. The sound was low, so there was a constant drone as background to our conversation. This sound would have been amplified for me if the hearing device had remained in my ear, but as soon as we were through the door I'd made an excuse to use the bathroom, and with some relief extracted the little cylinder, wrapped it tenderly in a tissue, and put it in my pocket.

Now we were sitting around like old friends. Innis was lolling in a leather sling-seat chair. Opposite him, Natalie and I sat demurely side by side on a stark black sofa that looked uncomfortable, but wasn't.

I'd already asked about the wine cellar. Innis had frowned, saying, "You don't want to go down there."

"Where is it, anyway?"

He'd waved vaguely in the direction of the kitchen, then stubbornly refused to say any more on the subject.

Speaking with the exaggerated precision intoxicated people use to hide their intoxication, Innis said, "Want to know how to in-ca-pac-i-tate" — he pronounced every syllable with great care — "a city like L.A.? Eh?" He paused, then answered his own question. "You frighten 'em. Make 'em panic, run for the hills."

"Is that what SHO's going to do?"

He looked at me blearily. "You know I can't say."

"Innis, how would *you* attack Los Angeles? Detonate a dirty bomb?"

The poor man's atomic weapon, the so-called dirty bomb was a conventional explosive around which was packed radioactive material. There was no atomic explosion, but the immediate area was sprayed with radiation. Relatively few people would be harmed. The damage would be primarily psychological. Radioactivity, invisible, intangible, was terrifying to most people, and they would flee any place they believed contaminated.

"Dirty bomb?" said Innis. His words were slurring quite noticeably now. He shook his head, then blinked hard, apparently dizzy. "Not a bomb. Something that would spread, and spread, and spread."

"Bioterrorism?" I asked. "Anthrax, maybe?"

He tried to focus on me. "Hmmmm," he said, in a vague affirmative. His eyes closed. A gentle snore followed.

"No head for alcohol," I observed.

Natalie grinned as she turned up the sound on the television set to drown out our conversation if indeed, anyone was bothering to listen. "No head for Rohypnol."

I looked at her, astonished. "You've given him a date rape drug?"

"Just enough to help him have a nice, long sleep. He'll be as good as new tomorrow. Help me get him onto his bed."

Shaking my head, I took his feet. "You amaze me." Together, with much effort, we manhandled Innis into his bedroom and laid him on his bed. Natalie took off his shoes and arranged him more comfortably. "He'll sleep the sleep of the innocent until tomorrow morning."

"The innocent?"

She made a face at my scathing tone. "You're right. The not so innocent."

We both looked down at his sleeping face. It was hard to imagine this man was a traitor to his country. Hell, in my book he was a traitor to civilization in general.

Tecla would be on full alert, waiting for Jason to come back from whatever it was that she had sent him to accomplish, so there was no point in trying to reconnoiter the house. Instead, I did a quick search to see if Innis had a mobile phone, explaining to Natalie my concerns about the credit card communication gismo. I was quite prepared to steal Innis's cell, if he had one, to give me a backup, but my larcenous ways were not required. He was phoneless.

Before we left the snoring Innis, I insisted we looked for the entrance to the wine cellar/bomb shelter. We found the trapdoor under a heavy, red woven rug in the hallway outside the kitchen. Not unexpectedly, the trapdoor was locked, and a quick search didn't turn up a key.

"What do you expect to find if you open it?" Natalie asked.

"There might be an alternative entrance to the property through the old bomb shelter."

"They'd have to come through a neighbor's place, wouldn't they?"

I'd already done a mental check of the information I had on the occupants of the houses adjacent to the Skinners' place. I told Natalie the FBI had run security profiles on everyone in the entire block, concentrating on the closest neighbors. No red flags had been raised.

"You'd think the most unobservant neighbors would still notice if people were sneaking through their back gardens, and disappearing underground," she said.

I had to acknowledge this was true. Getting down on my knees, I examined the lock. It seemed to be a substantial dead-bolt system. I didn't think it worth the risk to try opening it.

I put the rug back in position and dusted my hands. "Nothing more we can do, except . . ." I raised both eyebrows. Natalie elevated one.

"Excellent idea," she said. "My place, or yours?"

"Yours, I think. Perhaps we can put that shower to better use than before."

As soon as we were in Natalie's place, on went the television at high volume. It was irritating to have to worry about being overheard. I wasn't convinced the guest houses were bugged, but we both knew of agents in our profession who had come to unfortunate ends because of lack of due caution.

"If Tecla nabs us," I said, turning on the shower, "I'm going to claim that I was swept away by unexpected, overwhelming passion."

"A sound strategy," said Natalie, beginning to undress me. "For myself, I'll maintain you seduced me, and I was helpless to resist."

Our first — to this point our only — lovemaking had been in impossibly cramped surroundings, and even so had been sensational. "You remember our first time?" I said.

Natalie stepped out of the last of her clothes. "Only vaguely," she said against my mouth. "You'll have to refresh my memory."

The warm water poured over us. Locked in an embrace, we surrendered our vigilance, just for a few short, glorious minutes.

My body was taut with a growing, glowing, delightful discomfort. I closed around her fingers. "More, and deeper."

"Tyrant," she laughed.

On the brink, on the point of flight and fireworks. "Oh, darling," I gasped, then clenched my jaw to prevent myself from screaming out her name, as my body convulsed in her arms.

Spent, I slid to my knees. "You must suffer, as I have just suffered," I announced, throwing back my head. Water cascaded down the length of her and splashed into my face.

"Oh, please, yes," Natalie said.

Later, on the bed, I protested, "Again? My body may explode."

"I'm willing to take the chance, if you are."

"I'll hold you responsible."

She chuckled. "I'll *be* responsible."

My hips lifted involuntarily. My breath was laboring, as though I'd run a grueling race. My blood was singing as it zipped around my body. My heart? My errant heart was breaking, fracturing — just a little.

Amazingly, dangerously, we fell asleep in each other's arms, even though the light was on and the television was blaring in the other room. I awoke with a sickening shock about two in the morning. As I rolled out of the bed, Natalie's eyes opened. "Shh," I breathed, putting my hand over her mouth. She nodded to indicate she was fully awake.

"I heard something. A sharp bang — not a gunshot. Stay here." Seizing a light robe Natalie had left draped over a chair, I put it on, knotted the belt, then swiftly retrieved the little hearing device from my pocket, gathered the rest of my discarded clothes into an untidy bundle, and threw it into the bottom of Natalie's wardrobe.

I turned off the lights and the flickering television set. In the sudden silence I could discern the noise was coming from next door. I wondered for a moment if Innis had regained partial consciousness and was blundering around talking to himself, but then realized I could hear more than one person speaking.

Lurking like the neighborhood gossip at the front window, I peered out. Nothing was unusual. The moon was up, silvering the gardens and the pool area. The lights were still on in the main house, but no one seemed to be stirring.

I moved to the shared wall between the guest houses, placing my hearing gadget against the plaster. Voices jumped at me, as if next door a volume control had been abruptly turned too loud. Someone was swearing in Spanish. A second man, his tone sullen, was apologizing in the same language. Spanish wasn't one of my accomplishments, but I knew enough to work out that the angry man was berating someone else for allowing the trap door to slam. This must have been the noise that had jolted me awake.

Their voices went past me, moving in the direction of the front door. I whizzed over to the window again, and, like the femme fatale of some nineteen-forties crime movie, I flattened myself against the wall. Two men came out of Innis's place, each one carrying two metal attaché cases. Anthrax? Would they bring it here?

I watched them walk across to the house. The possibility one might be Red Wolf made me squint in the darkness, trying

124

to focus on anything I might find familiar, but in a few seconds they had disappeared into the house.

It was tempting to follow, but not only was I barefoot, and wearing only Natalie's flimsy robe, I couldn't come up with any reasonable excuse that would explain why I was padding around in the middle of the night, should I be discovered. I'd have to be patient. Tomorrow, as Scarlett O'Hara famously said, was another day.

I went back to Natalie, whispered to her what had happened, kissed her, and collected my clothes. Slipping out the door into the moonlight, I stood for a moment in the shadow cast by the edge of the building's tiled roof. It was such a beautiful, peaceful night. Far, far away a police siren wailed.

I looked over at the house. It seemed impossible to contemplate that within the next few days, perhaps even tomorrow, an attack would be masterminded from this place that would have the potential to destroy thousands of innocent people.

CHAPTER FOURTEEN

As it happened, I was wrong about the attack being masterminded from this particular house. Before breakfast we were all urgently summoned to the dining room. "All" in this case was me, Natalie, Gail and Innis, who looked thoroughly the worse for wear. He hadn't shaved, his clothes were crumpled, and his eyes were half-closed, as though the light was far too bright for him.

Gail, in comparison, was bright-eyed and more energized than I'd seen before. Hassling people apparently brought out the best in the woman. Earlier, she'd knocked on my guest house door with unnecessary force, and seemed disappointed to find I was already up and dressed. Natalie was also awake and alert, so Innis had provided Gail's first real challenge of the morning.

I'd come out to watch her in action. She pounded on his door, yelled his name, and generally made a hell of a fuss. The niggling worry that maybe the Rohypnol Natalie fed him had proved fatal was dispelled when, after a long delay, the door opened and Innis, wincing in the light, asked Gail in the rudest terms what she thought she was doing. She'd snarled a suitable reply, and stalked off, calling back over her shoulder, "And hurry up. Tecla says it's urgent."

It was clear this claim of urgency was no exaggeration. Tecla, dressed in faded jeans and denim shirt, was waiting in the dining room, Carmina by her side. Tecla's expression was bleak, her manner strained.

"I'm afraid," she said, "something has come up. We must immediately go to a contingency plan. Please return to your rooms and pack an overnight bag with essentials. If it becomes necessary, Carmina will follow later with the rest of your things."

"What the fuck's happened?" asked Innis, rubbing his forehead. He groaned. "Christ, I feel bad. I must have tied one on last night. Can't remember a thing."

His sister ignored him. "When you've packed, please come back here to the dining room. Carmina will provide coffee and bagels before we go."

Natalie asked, "Go where?"

Gail made an officious little noise to indicate she thought the question quite unnecessary.

Tecla said tersely, "We're relocating. Please hurry. I'll wait here for you."

Jason came in. He, too, was stony-faced, although where this made Tecla's features seem commonplace, his good looks were enhanced. Grim became him.

"It's agreed," he said to Tecla, "they'll follow this first contingent."

I didn't look at Natalie, but I knew what she was thinking. Red Wolf and whoever was with him would be leaving after us. If I could alert Artie Quillin and his special operations team, they could apprehend everyone in this second group as they left the Skinners' property.

And in that group would be Red Wolf.

No one showed more enthusiasm for packing an overnight bag than I did. Of course, in reality I was desperate to get back to my room, grab the credit card phone, and call my control, Ben. I had the cautious hope that this assignment could be wrapped up today, although a doubting inner voice pointed out this seemed too easy a resolution.

As soon as I was inside the guest house, I snatched the card out of my wallet, ready to take the chance that my call would be picked up by the monitoring system.

With my fingernail I punched in the pattern that should activate the automatic call sequence. Nothing. I tried again. And again. Nothing.

Either the card was inoperative, or the Skinners' security system electronically disrupted any attempt to call out.

Cell phones? I hadn't found a phone of any type in Innis's place last night, and although cells were omnipresent in the general public, I didn't recall anyone else in the house having one either. And it was no use trying to get a message out on the ordinary phone line. Tecla hadn't lied when she'd said the handsets required a punched-in code to get a dial tone. When, out of curiosity, I'd picked one up, there'd been dead silence.

Packing with speed, I crammed into my bag a change of clothes, toilet articles, and my makeup, including the mascara wand. Sighing, I put the hearing device in my ear. I was beginning to hate having random sounds amplified to wince level.

I popped in to see Natalie, who was also packed and ready to go.

"If I can get Tecla alone, I'm going to chat her up," I whispered in her ear, "so give me a little space before you come over. I reckon Innis will be ages getting himself together, but if he gets underway in the next few minutes, please head him off."

Natalie sent me a deeply reproachful look. "Chatting Tecla up? How soon you've forgotten our time together last night"

"Never!" I exclaimed, laughing. "Every detail is indelibly etched on my consciousness. Tecla is business, as you well know."

My luck was in. Tecla was alone in the dining room, listlessly eating a toasted bagel.

"Tecla," I said warmly, my tone intended to imply a closeness between us, "what's gone wrong? Can't you tell me why we have to get out of here?"

She considered me soberly, then, obviously swayed by my expression of keen, sympathetic interest, confided, "It's the FBI, and God knows what other agencies. We've had a contingency plan for this, but never thought we'd have to use it. We're moving you all to a new location, one that isn't known to the authorities." Her lip curled at this last word. "Motherfuckers," she said.

"But how did you find out this place was under surveillance?"

A struggle was apparent on her face. She wanted to tell me, but hadn't survived this long without learning that sharing information, unless absolutely necessary, was very unwise.

"Tecla," I said, a little wounded, "I've trusted my life to you. No strings. Can't you at least be honest with me?"

She paused, decided, said, "It was Gregory, Edward's chauffeur. Edward discovered he was a plant, an undercover agent, getting information to betray us."

"Jeez!" I shook my head. "Where's Gregory now? How can you stop him?"

Her expression was showed a trace of gratification. "This is a scenario we'd always envisaged as a possibility. We dealt with it."

Concealing the consternation that filled me, I said, "He's dead?" My tone was conversational.

Tecla raised one shoulder. "What choice did we have? The man knew too much, and was a danger not only to us, but to you, and all those other fighters for freedom who've trusted us."

My skin prickled, not just for Gregory and the horror he must have felt when he realized his cover was blown and he was going to die — but, selfishly, for myself. Gregory would certainly have known my real identity. Had he talked? Was Tecla just stringing me along, all the while knowing I, too, was a plant?

Hiding the tremor in my fingers, I selected a bagel, poured myself coffee, took the seat beside her. I said, offhandedly, "I hope you got something useful out of him before he died."

"Nothing. He held out, and then, there was no time." Tecla sounded irritated he'd proved so obstinate. "Jason disposed of the body in the L.A. National Forest overnight."

Even I had heard that the Los Angeles National Forest was the unauthorized cemetery of a thousand victims of criminal violence. "That's fine," I said, with moderate approval, "but surely his disappearance means you'll be given even more attention."

"The Feds won't know he's gone. Not yet. Edward's got everything at his end under control. Once they realize their agent isn't checking in, they'll certainly step up surveillance. That's why we're moving our base of operations now."

"But move where?" I asked, frowning. "Won't they just follow?"

A brief smile flickered across Tecla's lips. "We're well prepared, Diana, trust me. Edward has purchased several homes using different strategies, so it's impossible to trace anything back to him or any of his companies."

"But we'll be seen leaving, won't we?"

"No, we won't."

I nodded, showing satisfaction with the answer. I didn't ask how this would be achieved. I was sure I knew. Under the shelter of a spurious company name, Hydesmith had purchased the property behind the Skinners, and constructed the bolt hole through the bomb shelter.

I chewed a mouthful of bagel, swallowed it with some difficulty because my mouth was dry, then said, "Tecla? Who is it upstairs? I'm guessing someone important — someone working for our cause."

She turned her head sharply. "Don't ask."

I made an open-handed, trust-me gesture. "What do I have to do to prove I'm on your side? I believe what you believe. Why don't you understand that?"

I had to admit I was persuasive — I almost convinced myself. Tecla was close to succumbing, I could tell. All this was blown when my hearing gismo picked up heavy footsteps. Gail barged into the room, dumping her carry bag on the floor. Her expression changed as she took in the body language at the table, the two of us leaning toward each other in close conversation. It was obvious she resented my apparent intimacy with her boss.

Gail announced, loudly, "Jason says the transportation's ready."

Tecla pushed back her chair. "Tell Natalie and Innis they can forget breakfast. Get everyone moving, Gail, especially my dear brother." She glanced down at me. "You got Innis drunk last night."

"*I* got him drunk?" I said. "Hey, he was doing just the best job. He didn't need any help."

She nodded a reluctant assent. "You're right." Her face

darkened when she looked over at Gail, who hadn't moved. "Get your ass in gear! I want everyone ready to go in ten minutes."

As Gail, her mouth twisted with indignation, stomped out of the room, Tecla turned to me. "Later, Diana . . ." Her voice was softly suggestive. "I'd like you to stay longer in L.A. I know you have plans, but I have some too."

I was convinced sex figured largely in those plans, but I gave her my best puzzled, intrigued expression. "I'm not sure what you mean."

"We'll discuss it after this is over."

Innis dragged himself in after Natalie, who had tied back her heavy chestnut chair into a ponytail. Innis was sans his overnight bag, which made sense, as we would be exiting through his place. He'd made an attempt at shaving, and had nicked his chin. "Christ, I feel so bad . . ." He sat down, put his face in his hands, and groaned.

I thought, for a moment, Tecla was going to hit him. "You're fucking useless," she said, "all you ever —"

She broke off as Vin appeared in the doorway. "Tecla? You're wanted upstairs." He jerked his head for emphasis. As she complied, he looked me over, not appreciatively. Today Vin's hook nose and shadowed eyes seemed particularly predatory. I wondered what he'd been doing all night. Checking Red Wolf's team to ensure they were ready for the strike?

"Good morning, Vin," I said, suitably solemn to suit the occasion.

A flat stare and a grunt was my reward. I was fairly confident, given enough time, I could fully persuade Tecla I was true blue, but this guy? I'd have a snowball's chance in hell of winning him over.

* * * * *

Tecla came down carrying two of the silver attaché cases I'd seen last night. She was in a brisk, let's-get-things-done mood. I eyed the cases. Last night I'd theorized anthrax. This morning, looking at Tecla's tight hold on the handle, I wondered if it were money, and lots of it.

We made our way across the garden to Innis's guest house, looking rather like a little line of tourists about to join an all-expenses-paid bus trip. Tecla led, followed by Gail, who'd been given one of the silver attaché cases to carry, Natalie, Innis, and me. I glanced up at the sky, wishing with all my might that a helicopter, manned by intelligence agents, would be hovering overhead to note our odd procession. It was a faint hope. Ben had told me they'd decided to limit flyovers to avoid planting any suspicions that an eye in the sky was watching.

The mat was rolled back, the trap door open, revealing a flight of wooden steps. I checked the lock as I went down into the hole. A deadlock, with double bolts fitting into the steel surrounds of the trapdoor and needing a key to open either side.

There were wine bottles in racks at the bottom of the stairs. The rest of the area was bare. Rows of empty shelves were bolted to the reinforced concrete walls. There was a chill, dusty smell, and an odd deadness to any sounds. The lighting was dim. No one spoke, and even Innis hurried. It was as if we all pictured ourselves being buried here, underground, for good.

Since Tecla had told me of Gregory's death, I'd pushed the thought of his last hours out of my mind, but now my imagination came back with dreadful force. The thick concrete structure would muffle any sounds. Had they tortured him here? Killed him in these mean, chilly surroundings?

The old bomb shelter led to a new section, a narrow tunnel, reinforced with steel beams. There were lights at either end, but in the middle it was dark. Immediately claustrophobia grabbed me by the throat, making me so keen to get through to the other side that I bumped up against Innis.

"Hey," he said, with a touch of his usual jauntiness. "You coming on to me?"

"You had your chance last night," I said, "and you blew it." That shut him up.

The tunnel ended in the basement of the house Hydesmith had bought. I stopped to admire the door between the basement and the tunnel. The outer side was painted particle board, so when it was closed the door would be disguised as a wall of tools, each one meticulously placed in its correct, marked spot.

Jason was waiting for us upstairs in the kitchen, and also, to my surprise, was Edward Hydesmith, whose bloodshot eyes and drawn face indicated he probably hadn't slept at all last night. He was dapper as ever, however, with his white hair smooth, and his pale tan suit looking as though he'd just put it on fresh from the cleaners.

Apart from the Skinners and Hydesmith, no one seemed to know where to go or what to do. Innis chose to slump onto a kitchen stool and close his eyes. Gail planted herself beside Tecla, the very personification of a right-hand woman ready to lumber into action. Natalie leaned — very gracefully, I thought — against the sink.

I took the opportunity to look around, ostensibly curious about the kitchen, which had a solid, old-fashioned style, but actually taking the opportunity to use my enhanced hearing to sweep the area for any sound of interest. Nothing. Apart from our crowd in the kitchen, the house was empty.

Jason was obviously feeling the strain. He was shifting from foot to foot, moving his shoulders and stretching his neck. I kept my face blank, but inwardly I boiled with angry disgust. Last night in the hall Tecla had commanded Jason, "Get what you need, go with Edward, deal with it."

'Dealing with it' was actually Gregory's interrogation and

murder. I wondered what it was Jason had taken with him to accomplish the task. A weapon from the display case in his walk-in wardrobe? A length of wire for a garrote? And did Edward Hydesmith participate, or leave it all to Jason to carry out?

If appearances were true, Jason's nerves were snapping like old rubber bands, while Hydesmith's were in good shape. He smiled unctuously at Tecla, putting a manicured hand on her shoulder.

"It'll be all right, my dear," he said with a reassuring smile. "This is just a hiccup on the way to complete success. Indeed, it may turn out to be a blessing in disguise, as your location is further away from . . . any problem."

"Can we get going?" Jason blurted out. He tapped the face of his watch. "The other vehicles will be here, soon."

We collected our things and assembled outside the front door. Like the Skinners' residence, it had complete privacy, with a high hedge running along the edge of the property. Tall white gates separated the driveway from the outside street. The house itself was rather stodgy, sitting fat and heavy on the land. Indeed, if Gail had been a house, she'd be this one.

Parked by the front door were two vehicles. The first a corpulent SUV, white, with tinted windows; the second, a cream van with neat lettering along the side indicating it was owned by *Warhope & Sons, Exclusive Caterers*.

Hydesmith opened the back of the van, took out a white dustcoat and a baseball cap, and put them both on. The transformation was extraordinary. Tecla placed the silver attaché case in the SUV, then whipped out dark glasses and a colored scarf, which she expertly twisted around her head. I could never manage this, but was always lost in admiration at those who could. With a few deft twists, she'd wound the scarf in such a way that it suddenly became a fashion accessory.

Following Jason's instructions, Innis, Gail and I got in the van with Hydesmith, and Natalie clambered up into the back seat of the sports utility vehicle Tecla would be driving.

Natalie was going to have a much more uncomfortable trip than us. Gail, Innis and I would be seated on benches built into the back of the van, but Natalie would be traveling wedged on the floor between the front and back seats of the SUV.

We set off, Tecla and Natalie going first. Five minutes later, our van followed. Hydesmith drove, isolated in the front. The rest of us were in the back in a metal capsule that reminded me of a prison transport vehicle. Innis and Gail sat on one side, I occupied the bench opposite. The second silver case sat on Gail's lap with her hands resting on it protectively. I was revising my theory it contained money, as I couldn't see Tecla entrusting such wealth to Gail's care.

"What's in it?" I said, indicating the case.

She shook her head. "You don't need to know."

I didn't think I had much chance of charming the information out of her, so I turned to Innis. "Do you know where we're going?" I asked.

Innis shrugged. "Near UCLA campus. Don't have the address."

Gail had the smug manner of one who has secret, much-desired information. I said to her, "Tecla tells you everything, I suppose."

Gail swelled a little. "I'd say so."

Innis snorted. "Are you kidding me? You're a glorified gofer, Gail. Go for this, go for that. Tecla uses you every day in every way." He sat back, pleased with his summation.

Gail's lips thinned. "I won't bother telling you what you are, Innis."

"Innis," I said, intent on playing them off against each other, "you of all people know what's going on. How about sharing it with us?"

As I hoped, this was too much for Gail. "Shit! Innis wouldn't know his ass from his elbow."

"And *you* would?" Innis, still seriously hung-over, was getting royally pissed.

"I hear it's anthrax," I said. "The attack that's coming."

Gail took a breath, then pressed her lips together. "You know, don't you?" I injected a note of respectful admiration into my voice.

"Gail know?" Innis was contemptuous. "You're asking *her*?"

Desire to be the one privy to the secret information defeated Gail's common sense. "It isn't anthrax," she declared. "It's smallpox. I know that for a fact."

Chillingly, she patted the silver case as she spoke.

CHAPTER FIFTEEN

"Smallpox?" I said, interested, but not sounding alarmed. Gail nodded, self-importantly.

Innis was fed up. "You don't know when to keep your mouth shut," he said to Gail. She narrowed her eyes to slits, but kept a dignified silence.

Thank God, along with anthrax, I'd had a smallpox vaccination. I was one of the few in the world protected. The general public in the United States, I recalled, hadn't had mandatory vaccinations since the early nineteen-seventies. That meant the population had little or no resistance to this dreadful disease.

Smallpox. The very name caused a horror show of pictures to scroll across my mind: a baby crying weakly with pustules lining its mouth and throat; the disfiguring scabs on a young girl's face and arms, each one leaking fluid carrying virulent infection; the deep indented marks scarring a survivors' skin.

I ran through my last briefing on bioterrorism. Although smallpox had been declared eradicated worldwide in nineteen-eighty, the variola virus had not ceased to exist. Credible intelligence reports continued to surface that Russia had secretly produced smallpox virus in large quantities, in the process making it even more virulent and contagious with recombinant strains. The original smallpox had killed three in ten. This newer version would have a much higher death rate.

What tactics would Red Wolf use? Smallpox was spread by droplets released when an infected person coughed or sneezed, and by contact, skin to skin, or touching contaminated bedding or clothing. My background studies predicted bioterrorists would release the virus in aerosol form, which would disseminate widely in highly congested venues — a ballgame, entertainment complexes, an airport — anywhere attracting large quantities of people.

Sardonically, I congratulated Red Wolf on his timing. Released as an aerosol spray, the smallpox virus would be destroyed by high humidity and high temperatures, so summer in Los Angeles was out. Spring was ideal.

I had no doubt Red Wolf had the newer, more deadly version of the disease. The worst case estimate was that one infected person would in turn infect ten to twenty others. If he were to be inefficient, and only infect two hundred people in his initial smallpox attack, potentially that number could grow to between two thousand and four thousand people, and they in turn would infect third generation cases in an ever-widening circle of pain and death. Treatment at that point? None, except supportive therapy.

Strategies to cope once the attack had occurred? The idea was to step in early. It took twelve to fourteen days before high fever, headache and backache prostrated the victim. This was followed by a rash in mouth, throat, face, and forearms, spreading later to the rest of the body. Two days following, the characteristic pustules appeared, forming disfiguring scabs. At that point a laboratory could definitively confirm smallpox with an electron microscope examination of the pustular fluid.

The van swayed around a corner. A horn blasted. Up front, I heard Hydesmith swear. Innis and Gail studiously ignored each other. I looked vacantly at nothing in particular, my thoughts chattering in my head. Gail was holding a case that almost certainly contained smallpox virus on her lap. I'd surreptitiously checked, and there were two substantial combination locks that would be difficult to force open.

I'd seen four cases last night in the moonlight. It seemed prudent to have them transported separately, and as Tecla and Gail had two, I presumed the terrorists would have the other two. God knows how many pressurized aerosol cans each one contained. It was crucial I got the true nature of the attack out to Ben and Artie Quillin. They would alert O'Donnell and the individual bioterrorism teams.

The good news was the US government was holding enough doses of vaccine to cover most Americans, although those with compromised immune systems couldn't be vaccinated. The bad news was the first symptoms of smallpox were very like the flu, so, unless I alerted the authorities, thousands might die before the diagnosis of smallpox was even made.

I'd seen papers on responses to bioterrorism using smallpox as the weapon of choice. The overall approach was directed toward containment of an outbreak. It was the strategy that had defeated smallpox when it was a world scourge, a plan of "ring" vaccinations, as ever-widening circles of immunity are put in place to contain the infection. Vaccination, if given within two to four days of the original exposure, could prevent or lessen serious illness.

The effects of such an assault on the civilian population would not just be medical. I had seen an American doomsday report suggesting a major smallpox bioterrorism attack on a large urban center would not only cause widespread illness and death, but it would also shut down transportation and commerce in the area, literally costing the economy billions of dollars every week smallpox persisted.

The van jerked to a stop. Hydesmith might be many things, but a good driver wasn't one of them. "Out you get," he commanded, banging on the metal partition that separated us from the front compartment.

We grabbed our things and clambered out into a narrow laneway running behind a row of houses. I noticed Gail was holding the silver case so tightly her knuckles were white.

We were parked across a dilapidated double gate, but Hydesmith didn't bother opening it and parking inside. Instead he quickly shepherded us across a neglected back garden and into the house. From outside it looked like a comfortable, sprawling place, a little the worse for wear, but still holding its own. A quick glimpse of neighbors' residences suggested Hydesmith had purchased the worst property on the street, a sound business practice in real estate.

We trooped into the kitchen. Bringing up the rear, Hydesmith slammed the back door, ripped off his baseball cap and coat, and said tersely, "Ground rules. Don't go near any windows. Don't even think of leaving the premises. No phones, no talking to neighbors, no communication with anyone, anytime."

"Where's Tecla?" I asked. "And Natalie?"

"They took a longer, more circuitous route."

"And the others?" I inquired.

Edward Hydesmith smiled. It wasn't a happy curving of his lips, but a drawn back, death's head grin. "Little lady," he said softly, "you'll get your tits ripped off, if you're not very careful."

"Oh, ouch," I said, taking the threat as a light-hearted comment, although it wasn't.

Gail, affronted, glared at him. Innis scowled, and although I would have liked to think he was outraged on my behalf, I rather suspected his negative response was to Hydesmith's coarseness, rather than to the attempted intimidation in his words.

I wandered off to explore the place, heading for the front of the house to get as far away as possible from Edward Hydesmith. I'd become skilled at hiding my real feelings, but this time I was so coldly angry that I feared he would read it in my face. The last thing I wanted was for him to consider I was in any way a threat.

Peering through the narrow beveled glass windows set into the top half of the heavy front door, I could see the house was built on a slope, which necessitated many steps leading up from the street below. A steep driveway led to a large garage, with room for three vehicles. I entered it from an internal stairway and found nothing exciting, just a wooden bench holding a few tools, a pile of flattened cardboard cartons, and a car — a brown sedan of uncertain age, parked with its nose to the roller door. The key was in the ignition, as if ready for a getaway. I checked the fuel gauge. Full to the top. The tires were almost new. On a hunch I opened the bonnet and had a look at the engine compartment. As I'd suspected, the shabby, neglected exterior held a well-maintained motor.

I went to the bottom of the stairs and listened. Thanks to my gismo, I was confident no one was nearby. Slipping the tiny cardphone out of the hip pocket of my jeans, I punched in the code, and listened. This time it wasn't quite dead, as I could hear soft electronic clicks. But that was all. I was out of range.

For a moment I considered slipping out the front of the house and down the drive. I saw myself pounding on someone's door and begging to use the phone. This being the States, the homeowner's response would probably be to call the cops. And by the time I'd finally got to Ben, Red Wolf would be long gone.

Putting that plan on hold, I considered my next move, which was clearly to wait at least until my quarry was definitely in the house. Of course, there was always the chance he wasn't coming here at all, and had been taken somewhere else entirely. I sighed. If I kept this up I would talk myself into a serious despondency.

High priority was constructing a mental floor plan of this building, so I concentrated on that. A narrow hall ran from the front door back to the kitchen. There were two levels — three, if you counted the garage. Two bedrooms were in the front, the larger one being above the garage. These bedrooms shared a bathroom tiled in bilious green, partnered with a truly horrific bright purple, nylon shower curtain.

The next level, dictated by the sharp incline, was several steps up, and contained two more bedrooms, a second bathroom — brown and orange this time — a largish living room, and a formal dining room with a separate guest toilet nearby. The kitchen, through which we'd entered the house, had a breakfast nook that looked like a fun place to sit and read the paper. Adjoining was a laundry room.

The house had no patio, no veranda, no sundeck. And no phones. In several rooms I'd seen the plug-in connections in the walls, but a quick look in nearby drawers and cupboards didn't turn up any handsets.

The house was fully furnished in the most boring, unimaginative way possible. It was a timewarp dwelling, its staid furniture, wallpaper, window treatments and overall color schemes reminding me strongly of my grandmother's house, which I'd last seen years ago.

Coming back to the kitchen, I looked around and decided my gran would have been right at home in this room. She'd had a breakfast nook just like this one, with similar orangey Formica on the table top. She'd had rows of kitchen cupboards almost identical to these ones, although hers had been green, not brown. She'd had the same restricted bench space, strip lighting and single-bowl, stainless steel sink.

I was gratified to see Hydesmith and Innis sitting in the nook making a list of supplies to feed us all, and even more gratified to find that Gail was talking on a mobile phone, apparently being exempt from Hydesmith's no phone policy.

"She isn't here yet, Jason," Gail was saying. "Okay, I'll call back the moment she arrives."

Gail flipped the phone closed and shoved it in the pocket of her slacks. So she hadn't borrowed it from Hydesmith — it was hers. Now my chances of calling out from here were considerably enhanced. Gail had a phone. Jason had one too.

My amplified hearing picked up the sound of the garage door opening, which almost certainly indicated Natalie and Tecla had made it safely here. No one else heard anything, so a few moments later, when a door slammed in the front of the house, Hydesmith started. In a smooth movement he was on his feet, in his hand a handgun snatched from a belt holster at the small of his back.

I recognized the weapon. It was a Smith & Wesson silver and black semiautomatic in the Sigma Series, ten-round capacity.

"Edward?" called Tecla.

Hydesmith relaxed. "We're here, in the kitchen," he announced, shoving the gun back into its holster.

Things were looking up. Now I knew Hydesmith carried a gun, and I was fully confident I could take it from him. From now on I was expecting Jason, too, would be armed with at least one of those cherished weapons he'd collected. Tecla? Maybe. Gail? I gave her body a furtive once-over as she retrieved her cell phone to call Jason back.

The loose top she wore could hide more than one weapon, but somehow I couldn't see the Skinners arming her. But then, why not? She'd been assessed by intelligence as fanatically loyal. Upon reflection, I doubted she die for Jason, but for Tecla . . . she might.

Natalie and Tecla joined us in the kitchen, Tecla carrying her silver case, which she set carefully down beside Gail's.

Perhaps because he felt entitled, as he owned the house,

144

Edward Hydesmith was very much in charge. "From this point on, the front bedrooms, the bathroom next to them, and the garage underneath are not to be entered. Is that clear?" He waited until everyone assented before he went on. "The back two bedrooms, the living room and the bathroom are yours. Divide them up any way you like."

Wanting to be somewhere that would allow me to move around without disturbing anyone else, I said — quite inaccurately, I hoped — "I snore, so I'll take the couch in the living room."

It was agreed that Tecla and Jason were to take one room, with Innis sleeping on the floor on a bed constructed of cushions taken from lounge chairs. Gail and Natalie would share the other bedroom.

Tecla and Gail went off in the white SUV to buy supplies. Hydesmith disappeared to move the van from the back lane to street parking. Innis, obviously still suffering from the effects of last night, arranged himself in the nook and closed his eyes.

Taking this opportunity, I showed Natalie over the house, and together we examined possible escape routes: the front door, of course, although it had been fitted with a new deadbolt, the garage had old-fashioned roller doors that I'd already noticed made a hell of a noise, the back door to the kitchen, which also had a new deadbolt fitted, a door in the laundry that led to a side passage — as an oversight, this hadn't been fitted with a new lock. And, at a pinch, there were several windows on both sides of the house with short drops to the ground.

"I'm not keen on sharing a double bed with Gail," murmured Natalie, surveying the back bedroom designated for the two of them. She kept her voice low, although we'd agreed it was highly unlikely this house was bugged, there was no reason to take chances.

"She probably snores," I said, grinning. "If it's too much for you, come out and join me on the couch."

145

I winced as the back door slammed, reverberating through my head as the sound was magnified in my left ear. Edward Hydesmith apparently had never learned to close a door quietly. I heard him say something sharp to Innis, and Innis reply in a irritable tone.

I whispered to Natalie, "I'm going to give you a telephone number to call, just in case you get the opportunity, and I don't."

I'd already broken regulations by telling Natalie anything at all about my assignment, and was breaking a couple more by giving her the emergency access number. I figured this situation trumped any rules about confidentiality. And I trusted her, totally, which was more than I could say for Lawrence O'Donnell and his lot.

She repeated the number to me twice, then nodded. "Got it. There's a password, I suppose."

"Wombat's testicles."

Natalie smirked. "Your choice, I imagine?"

"Oh, here you are," said Hydesmith, putting his head through the bedroom door. "It'd be a help if you made up the beds for everyone. The stuff's in the closet over there."

"Shall we make up the front rooms too?" I asked sweetly.

He hesitated, then said, "Why not? Do them first, though, and hurry."

There were twin beds in each of the front bedrooms. As we stripped off the dingy bedspreads — the four had identical brown and dark green patterns — Natalie said, "I worked as a chambermaid in a London hotel, years ago in my impoverished student days. Hard work and badly paid."

I looked at her affectionately, wondering if we'd ever have time to relax and while away the time swapping stories about our lives. "Meet any lords and ladies?"

"Scads of them. Moth-eaten bunch." She looked with disdain at the selection of sheets we'd unearthed. "Where do you think these came from? Kitsch city?"

It was a nauseous assortment. Of particular note was a

striped set of mustard and chocolate brown sheets, although a pink and mauve floral number came close.

With the tension release of silliness, we chortled as we made up the beds with sheets and pillowcases we'd assessed as the worst and most visually disturbing of the bed linens available.

We were just tucking the last bedspread into place when Innis appeared. "Tecla and Gail are back with the groceries. Edward says to come and help put them away."

He surveyed the room with a curled lip. "What a dump this joint is. And Edward's acting like it's a fucking palace, and he's the fucking king."

"How long are we stuck here?" I said, with a hint of a complaining whine in my voice. "I mean, there isn't even a swimming pool." Natalie nodded agreement, and we both looked expectantly at Innis.

"Tomorrow's the day," he said. It was plain he'd given up any pretence of discretion. "I guarantee it'll be a Monday L.A. will never forget."

"So we can go back to Beverly Hills after tomorrow?"

"That's the plan." He added with a sly smile, "Wouldn't count on going shopping for a while, though. Could be very unhealthy for you."

Three things I didn't know a minute ago, I thought as we followed Innis back to the kitchen. *The attacks start tomorrow. Beverly Hills shopping center is one of the targets. If we're moving back to the house, it's likely Red Wolf will be well on his way out of the country.*

Tecla had parked the SUV in the back yard. She and Gail trotted to and fro until they'd unloaded all the supermarket bags. I volunteered to help, as I wanted to have another look at the lane and the neighboring houses, but Hydesmith barked "No, absolutely not," and put me and Natalie to work putting everything away.

"Don't men have grocery-relocation skills?" I asked sarcastically, looking pointedly at Hydesmith and Innis.

147

"Just do it," Hydesmith, rolling his eyes with a can-you-believe-this-bitch look.

This pleased me. He was already taking me for granted. I hoped very much he would come to regret it, deeply.

Half an hour later everything was put away and we were all enjoying coffee in an assortment of chipped mugs. It was surprisingly good, considering it had been made in an extremely ancient coffee percolator.

Innis had just asked disconsolately if there was any alcohol. Tecla had had great satisfaction replying in the negative, when Gail's phone rang. She fished it out of her pocket, listened, then handed it to Tecla, who said, "Right, we're on our way to meet you."

Handing back the cell to Gail, she said to Hydesmith, "That was Jason. They're just coming up the drive."

"Excellent." Hydesmith was suddenly affable. "Come on, Tecla my dear, let's make them welcome."

He picked up the silver cases and was about to leave the kitchen when he swung around to say, "Natalie, Diana? We have a special guest, as you no doubt know. His identity is no business of yours. Let me make one thing very clear. If you see his face, you die. Simple as that."

CHAPTER SIXTEEN

Dinner was pasta and meat sauce, cooked by Gail with assistance from Natalie. I offered help, but was rejected with a cold look from Gail, who seemed to take my overture as a criticism of her abilities.

Tecla, Jason and Hydesmith came back to eat with us. Jason, I noticed with cynical amusement, had a cowboy swagger, caused no doubt by the gun he had holstered on his hip. He also carried a shotgun, which he set down carefully beside him when he ate.

Vin came back to collect food for Red Wolf and his party. His cold, indifferent glance passed over us all, including his eager fellow-travelers, Tecla and Jason. It seemed to me that if necessary, he would execute us all without a pang.

I noticed with interest there were four plates on the tray he took with him. When he didn't return, I surmised that the food was for himself, Red Wolf, plus two others, probably the men I'd seen carrying the cases into the Skinners' house last night.

Without a television set, or even a radio, the evening stretched bleakly ahead. I was tempted to mention a game of charades, but for once discretion got the better of me. I did manage to have a quick conversation with Natalie while we were washing the dishes. This was clearly a macho household.

Having done a quick check of the kitchen drawers, I knew there were no sharp knives of any description. In fact, there was nothing that could be used as an effective weapon. I murmured to Natalie, "Any Rohypnol left?"

She looked demure. "A little. What did you have in mind?"

"I'm not sure. Just canvassing possibilities."

"It's in with my makeup, disguised as a bottle of eyedrops."

"Sneaky." I looked over my shoulder at Edward Hydesmith, who was deep in conversation with Tecla, patting her knee every now and then. What a creep.

About nine o'clock Jason went up front, returning shortly with Vin and three silver attaché cases. Gail leapt up, grabbed the keys to the SUV, and led the way outside. A few minutes later I heard the engine roar. Jason returned alone.

"Gone for an evening drive?" I said.

He grinned, superior in his knowledge of what was going on. "You could say that."

Shortly afterward, Vin came back to collect Tecla, Jason and Hydesmith. Apparently there was to be a council of war. Before departing, Tecla had a whispered conversation with Innis, glancing every now and then in our direction.

After they'd gone, Innis got up, checked the back door, and then settled himself in the breakfast nook, which was fast becoming his favorite nest. "This is so bloody boring," he said, his eyes drooping. He yawned. "Come and entertain me."

Natalie said to me in a low voice, "While I was putting things away I found a couple of bottles in the cupboard above the sink."

"Cooking sherry?"

"Something like that. Possibly Innis might be interested in a nightcap . . ."

There was a half bottle of sherry, one of port, and, extraordinarily, a bottle containing amber liquid labeled *Genuine Mead*.

I plunked them all on the table in front of Innis, got three tumblers, and sat down with Natalie opposite him. Innis's eyes lit up. "Well, *hello*, where did this come from?"

He announced the mead was too damn sweet, but quaffed it anyway. Natalie and I sipped decorously, Innis sampled the sherry, made a face, but finished a tumbler of that too. "You know," he said, his mouth twisting, "I'm treated like a bloody servant. Tecla and Jason have just decided they're leaving tonight to fly to Aspen, in Edward's private jet, naturally, while I'm left to baby-sit you."

"Odd time to decide to go skiing," I said.

"Sort of an alibi," said Innis, inspecting his empty glass. "When the shit hits the fan here in L.A., they'll be off with the beautiful people."

Natalie poured a large measure of port into his tumbler. "Is Edward Hydesmith going too?"

Innis blinked slowly, trying to focus on her face. "Edward fancies himself a power player," he said with envy, mixed with derision. "Without his money he'd be nothing, nobody."

He tossed back the port, gagged a little, then licked his lips. In a few minutes his head was on his folded arms, and he was snoring gently.

"Did you slip him something?" I asked.

Natalie spread her hands. "Not a thing. That port must have quite a kick."

I slid out of the seat. "I'm going down the front. Start a loud conversation with Innis if Vin and Gail turn up. I'll hear you easily, and get the hell out of there."

The hallway was lit only by one dim light. The doors to both bedrooms and the stairs that led down to the garage were all closed. I listened, hearing Tecla's lighter tones above the masculine voices. It seemed they were all in the larger bedroom. To make sure, I listened at the other door, then opened it cautiously. The light was on, but there was no one there. A single silver case lay on the bed nearest the door. I rapidly checked it. Locked.

A quick look through the narrow windows of the front door showed a vehicle parked at the top of the drive outside the garage. With only the street lights below providing faint illumination, I couldn't tell its color, but it looked like a black or navy BMW sedan.

Somebody laughed in the room to my right. It was impossibly dangerous, but I crouched down to listen at the door, telling myself if I sensed that someone was coming to open it, I had time to make the only close bolthole, the stairs leading to the garage. I had left that door slightly ajar.

In total I could distinguish six voices, though three were dominant, Hydesmith's, Tecla's, Jason's, and a light, accented male voice. Red Wolf. The two other men made only a few comments. The language of choice was mainly English, although now and then Tecla and Red Wolf slipped into French.

My knees cramped, my back hurt, but I didn't move, transfixed by what I was hearing. They discussed the targets and the expected casualties in pragmatic, businesslike tones. As far as I could tell, there were eight separate targets. Three were shopping centers — Beverly Hills, and two huge shopping complexes, one in Orange County, one in the Valley, "To be even-handed," said Tecla with a laugh.

In downtown Los Angeles — one office tower, a court

building, and Parker Center, the core of the L.A. Police Department.

To finish off the list, two major hospitals, deliberately chosen as they were both designated as central medical centers in the case of a terrorist attack.

In most cases the aerosol spray containing the smallpox virus would be released into the air-conditioning. In addition, in the stores, aerosol sprays would be used to saturate goods and clothing on racks. This would be the preferred method on Rodeo Drive.

I wasn't sure how many men Red Wolf had in the field, but it was obvious they had been well-prepared for some time in advance, as their ease of entry into the air-conditioning facilities was taken for granted. Vin, driven by Gail, who was familiar with the roads, was apparently distributing the smallpox canisters to managers in each area, who would in turn distribute them to the team members entrusted in delivering the virus to the selected sites.

Beverly Hills was to be given special treatment, with Red Wolf's two aides carrying out the contamination under Vin's personal direction. The total number of victims, as Jason pointed out, would be comparatively small, but the impact of an attack on such a world famous area would be considerable.

Everything was to be coordinated by Red Wolf, assisted by Hydesmith. Eleven in the morning had been decided as the optimum hour, but the exact time would be determined by Red Wolf. All operatives carried pagers, and would not release the virus until they were activated by a message in code. Red Wolf, his voice soft, but with a whiplash authority, made it clear no one would act without his express command. In the unlikely event there was a problem, a pager message would be sent to advise what action to take.

There was a general sound of movement in the room, as though people were getting up to leave. With difficulty I straightened up. A cramp bunched the calf muscles of one leg. It hurt like hell, but I bounded down the hallway, skidded into the guest bathroom near the dining room, shut the door, turned on the light, flushed the toilet, then turned on the water in the basin full bore.

I leaned on the basin, breathing like a serious asthmatic. My face in the mirror was a yellowy white. Terror did not become me.

After gulping down a mouthful of water, I dried my hands, smoothed down my hair, and opened the door. Tecla was just passing. "Diana, I thought you'd be in bed by now."

I made a face. "I would be, except Innis kept on talking, and then we found a couple of bottles, and basically, had a little party."

Tecla's expression soured. "Oh, shit," she said, stalking off toward the kitchen. I followed, to find her, hands on hips, standing over Innis, who was staring blearily up at her.

Natalie, still sitting where I'd left her, looked apologetic. "I think it was the mead," she said. "Innis says he feels sick."

As if on cue, Innis put his hand to his mouth and made a clumsy dash for the bathroom. "Oh, shit," said Tecla again.

I went to bed on the couch. I'd wondered if Tecla would be kind and point out I could use the bedroom set aside for her and Jason, but as Innis, who'd vomited violently, was now passed out on the double bed, I wouldn't have taken her up on it anyway.

Around two o'clock, Vin and Gail came in through the kitchen. Tecla had a whispered conversation with them, but as I'd taken out the hearing device and turned it off to conserve the battery, I couldn't make out what she was saying. A few minutes later she and Jason left through the back. I heard a loud click as the deadbolt was engaged, and after a short pause I heard the SUV start. Vin walked heavily down the hallway to the front bedrooms, and Gail thumped around in the bathroom for ages, before going to bed.

Feigning sleep, I ran through the personnel in the house. Vin, Red Wolf, Hydesmith and two other men were in the front bedrooms. Innis was unconscious in one of the back bedrooms. Natalie was probably awake in the other bedroom, and Gail, who I could now hear snoring, was asleep in the same room.

Light footsteps moved along the hallway. In the half-lit living room I tensed on the couch, but kept my eyes shut and my breathing even. I sensed someone looking in, and opening my eyes the merest slit, saw it was Edward Hydesmith.

He paused for a long moment, then continued down to check on Natalie and Gail. When I heard Innis's sleepy, complaining voice, I decided Hydesmith was going to have at least a few hours rest on a bed, and Innis was taking up more than his fair share.

I was considering getting up and trying the laundry door, when I heard more footsteps in the hall. Two men passed in the dim light, talking softly to each other. From their voices, neither was Red Wolf.

I heard the scrape of a chair, the sound of a match, then the long sigh of a smoker enjoying a first hit of nicotine.

Getting up was no longer an option.

I lay still, working on possible plans of action. All had glaring holes and every chance of failure. Even if I could get out and phone Ben, Red Wolf would have time to activate his team to contaminate thousands of victims.

It would be better to give Natalie the responsibility of calling, and deal with Red Wolf myself. A nice plan, but how in the hell to achieve it? Tomorrow morning, when Vin and the two other members of the team had departed the house,

I would be left with four people to worry about. Even with Natalie's help, somehow we had to overcome Gail, Innis, Hydesmith and Red Wolf. Simple really . . .

My heart quivered. In a few hours I might very likely die.

CHAPTER SEVENTEEN

The problem of Gail solved itself. She was going to chauffeur Vin and the two other guys in the catering van, which had been parked on the street since yesterday afternoon. They left the house at nine. Now there were three: Red Wolf, Hydesmith and Innis. The first two were certainly armed. I was sure Innis was not. No one would trust him with a loaded weapon.

I snatched a moment to tell Natalie what I was proposing to do about Red Wolf, and she looked suitably appalled. "What are you going to arm yourself with?"

I indicated the hip pocket of my jeans. "I have my mascara wand blade."

She rolled her eyes. "Oh, terrific. That'll be effective against a bullet."

I'd hoped Jason would forget his shotgun, but it had disappeared, so either he'd taken it with him, or it was in the front room. "Hydesmith's carrying a semiautomatic," I said. "The holster's in the small of his back."

"And he'll hand it over if you ask?"

"Probably not. I'll improvise. Your eyedrops come to mind."

"What about Innis?"

"I don't think he's armed." I slipped her a piece of paper, torn from an old magazine I'd found. "The list of targets," I said. "The moment you can, call Ben. Tell him Red Wolf activates his team at eleven. If I don't stop him before he sends the signal, at least a quarantine can be thrown around each site."

"Hydesmith will have a cell phone," she said with confidence, putting the list into her shirt pocket. "I imagine it'll be the very latest, and smallest."

"This is going to blow your cover, if you're seen to be helping me."

Natalie gave me a wry smile. "Can't be helped."

She broke off as Edward Hydesmith appeared, followed by Innis. Hydesmith was as nattily dressed as always, Innis's clothes were creased and his face unshaven.

"You don't look well," I said to Innis. He groaned.

Hydesmith ignored him and concentrated on me and Natalie. "Coffee," he commanded. His view of women seemed old-fashioned, and I told him so.

"Oh, I'll make the coffee," said Natalie, impatient with us both. "Do you want toast, too?"

"Dry toast for me," said Innis.

Hydesmith shot him a look of corrosive dislike. "You're supposed to be guarding the back of the house. Is that too big a job for you?"

Innis put up one hand. "All right, all right . . ." He shook his head to clear it, then, from his expression, was sorry that he'd shaken it.

"Do you want coffee for whoever's in the front, too?" Natalie asked, starting the percolator.

"No. Just me. Cream and two sugars," he said, sitting down as if this were a coffee shop and we were the staff.

"Are my eyes bloodshot?" I inquired.

Natalie peered at me. "They certainly are. I've got some eyedrops, if you like."

Even in this situation, I hid a smile when she turned her back to the men and winked at me.

When I returned with the eyedrop bottle hidden in my hand, Natalie was pouring coffee into four mugs. I had no idea how strong this Rohypnol in liquid form was, but there wasn't much left, so I decided to give the whole lot to Hydesmith and deal with Innis some other way.

It took longer than I expected. Hydesmith was on his second cup of coffee when he put a hand to his head, a puzzled look on his face. He half stood up, then sat down again, hard. After a moment he toppled sideways onto the floor.

Innis slid out of the breakfast nook and leaned over to regard Hydesmith's unconscious body with owl-like astonishment. "What's wrong with him?"

I checked my watch. It was nearly ten. I was bending to pull up Hydesmith's jacket and seize the gun, when I heard a metallic click. I'd been wrong about Innis. He *had* been trusted with a firearm. It was a little thing — a snub-nosed automatic, probably only good at short range, but that was all that was needed here.

"The safety's off," he said, blinking hard. He took a deep breath. "Don't move, either of you."

I straightened up. He was within easy reach.

"What in the hell is this about?" Natalie demanded. "Put the gun down, for heaven's sake."

His expression obstinate, he snapped, "Don't tell me what to do. You've given something the Hydesmith to knock him out."

Natalie flicked a glance at me, then extended her hand to Innis. "Hand it over, Innis. Stop fooling around."

He glared at her, opened his mouth to speak. With one swift movement I snatched the knife from my hip pocket and swept it in a shallow arc, driving the wickedly thin ceramic blade deep into his forearm. It grated on bone, then went straight through. Innis gave a bleat of surprised horror as the bloody tip appeared, piercing his silk shirt.

I caught the gun as it slipped from his fingers and tossed it to Natalie. Innis whimpered, "My arm." He sat down, cradling his injury. "You stabbed me," he said in a tone of incredulity. His face was putty-colored as he tugged at the blade.

"Don't pull it out," I advised. "You'll do more damage."

Wrenching the gun out of Hydesmith's holster, I checked the magazine and put a round in the chamber ready to fire. "I'll go for Red Wolf," I said to Natalie. "Phone as soon as you can."

Innis's head jerked up. "You know his name? Jesus, what else do you know?"

Natalie said, "I'll deal with Innis. You go."

From the front of the house came the sound of a substantial door slamming. The front door. Innis managed a faint, sardonic smile. "Bad luck. You've missed him. He always intended to be on the move when he sent the coded messages."

I raced down the hallway, skidded to a stop at the front door. Through the panes I could see the figure of a man opening the door of the BMW, which was still parked at the top of the drive. I opened the door a crack, catching a glimpse of a white T-shirt, black jeans, and a black baseball cap. In the daylight the car was dark blue, not black.

He slammed the door, the engine started, and in an instant he was backing rapidly down the drive. The car was brand new — it had no number plate, but only the name of the dealer who'd sold it.

I raised the gun. On foot I couldn't catch him, and even if I tried a shot from the front steps, the chances I'd hit him weren't good.

A moment's wait to see which way he turned on the street, and then I was leaping down the stairs to the garage. The brown car? Was it still there?

It was sitting where I'd first seen it, facing outward for a quick getaway. I slapped the switch to activate the roller door, jammed the gun into the waist of my jeans, flung myself into the driver's seat, gunned the motor, and had it moving as soon as I thought I had a chance to clear the rising door.

As it was, I scraped the roof and lost the radio antenna, but I was out and zooming down the steep drive, my tires squealing as I turned up the hill, the way the BMW had gone.

I raced along the suburban road, praying I'd catch sight of Red Wolf's vehicle before it was lost in a maze of streets. And also praying I'd remember to stay on the right side of the road. In Australia we drove on the left. "Keep right, keep right," I chanted to myself.

Far up ahead were red traffic lights, where the street met a main thoroughfare. As I accelerated toward them they turned green. I caught a glimpse of navy blue car turning left. I smashed my hand on the horn, swerving around someone unwise enough to pull out of a driveway without checking it was clear.

The lights turned red again before I hit the intersection, but I didn't brake. Turning left in a sliding skid, I narrowly missed a bus. Worse, I nearly turned to the wrong side of the road, where vehicles were already rolling toward me. The rear fishtailed as I over-corrected, then I was running straight again, leaving the blasts of irate horns behind me.

The shabby brown sedan I was driving had a surprising acceleration. I wove in and out of the traffic, searching for a dark blue sedan. Drawing close to one of the correct color, I

161

found the driver a tiny, grim-faced woman, who gave me a belligerent glare when I peered into her vehicle.

I speeded up, whipped past her, stole a quick glance at my watch. Ten-forty. Then, there he was! Fifty meters ahead of me, a blue BMW was making a right. I roared up to the intersection, braked hard, and turned. Signs indicated I was entering UCLA. Red Wolf clearly intended to lose himself in the University of California's extensive grounds.

He hadn't stopped at the parking kiosk, so apparently he didn't intend to use one of the parking structures. Almost immediately I was forced to jolt to a precipitate stop, obeying the red light at a T-junction. Students, chattering like birds, crowded the crossing in front of me. I swung my head both ways. There he was, disappearing up to the right.

"Emergency! Emergency!" I shouted through the window, ignoring the red light and butting my way through throngs of students. One slapped the car hard and yelled something insulting, but I got free without actually running anyone down.

Ahead, the rear lights on Red Wolf's vehicle glowed. I was sure he hadn't seen me — if he had, would he be slowing down? Infuriatingly, another stream of students meandered across the a pedestrian crossing in front of me. I shot through a gap, accelerated, then stamped on the brake.

Red Wolf had parked his car and was walking away from it. In a moment, a clump of students had swallowed him up.

CHAPTER EIGHTEEN

I didn't bother with the niceties of parking. I left the brown sedan, door open, motor running, and took off after him. I kept my hand over the gun rammed into the waist of my jeans, fearing that some macho kid might try to stop me if it were clearly visible. Besides, it was a double-action automatic, and I had put a round into the chamber, so it was ready to fire. I didn't like to contemplate what would happen if I jolted the trigger and it accidentally discharged.

No one seemed surprised to see me running. Perhaps it was taken that I was late for class. I was in some sort of plaza, dotted with fine old trees. I absently noted a huge Morton Bay Fig from Australia. Dodging knots of people, I bolted across the plaza, desperately scanning for a white T-shirt, black jeans, black baseball cap. Hell, every second male seemed to be wearing something similar.

How could I be sure I'd know his face? I could have run past him, and not realized. I stopped, the breath sobbing in my throat. Ahead was a wide, grassed quadrangle, surrounded by imposing buildings.

Look for someone alone, someone without a briefcase or a pack.

My gaze focused on one man, medium height, strolling away from me. The way he walked, the way he held his head — for a moment I was transported to a dark, rain-swept dock. As I watched, he stopped at a flight of shallow steps, leaned negligently against the railing, and reached into his pocket.

I wrenched the automatic out of my waistband. Someone nearby exclaimed. I ran toward Red Wolf, students scattering before me. His head was bent, examining something in his hand. A guy yelled, "She's got a gun!" Red Wolf looked up.

How could I have thought I'd not recognize his face? "You're Red Wolf," I said. "Drop the phone."

We were of a height, so we stood eye to eye. I held the gun in both hands in the approved manner. He ignored the weapon. "And you are?"

"You don't need to know."

He narrowed his eyes. "The Australian," he said. "On the boat."

In the distance I heard a siren. UCLA, I recalled, had its own police force. I could only hope they'd listen to me first, before shooting.

"Drop the phone," I said. "Now. Then put your hands behind your head and sit down. Slowly. If you go for your gun, I'll kill you."

He didn't move. His was an ordinary, pleasant face. Not the face one would put on a mass murderer.

"Let's talk about this, okay?"

It was a classic technique: get your opponent to debate you. I said, "Drop the bloody phone."

"If you insist. Can I put it down? I don't want to break it."

"Drop it!"

Red Wolf seemed about to comply, then he moved suddenly, violently, flinging the cell phone at my face. Before I could fire, he leapt at me, his hands seizing my wrists. We wrestled, his contorted face close to mine. Someone screamed. No one came to help.

He was amazingly strong. In a moment, he would overcome me, kill me without compunction, grab the phone and send the signal to release the smallpox.

"Give up, you bitch," he ground out, trying to twist the gun from my fingers.

I took a huge breath and used every bit of strength I had to force the barrel down. I'd like to say I had a moment's qualm before I pulled the trigger, a jolting realization that I was at once both judge and executioner.

None of that happened. I simply fired. Killed Red Wolf with one shot in the center of his ordinary face.

CHAPTER NINETEEN

"Shall we swim, or just lie here doing nothing?" asked Siobhan/Natalie.

"I vote for lying here doing nothing."

We were in a true tropical paradise in the Caribbean, an island resort so exclusive that it was never advertised, but relied on recommendations from its clientele.

I could never have afforded this luxury, but Siobhan's father had insisted that we take a total break for at least a couple of weeks. I hadn't even made a token protest.

Back in the real world, the United States intelligence services had received grateful accolades from the president down to the ordinary person in the street. I'd seen countless television sound bites of Lawrence O'Donnell pontificating about the professionalism of the men and women who laid their lives on the line to protect their country. Credit, in a vague way, was given to "foreign intelligence services" who had provided valuable support in this foiling of a potentially devastating bioterrorism attack.

Neither Siobhan nor I expected, or indeed could allow ourselves, to be named. I looked across at her and smiled, remembering that morning. With the UCLA police advancing across the quad, weapons drawn, I'd tossed away my gun, grabbed Red Wolf's phone and punched in the emergency number. Ben answered immediately, telling me Siobhan had already called in the alarm, and the entire might of law enforcement and every available intelligence agent was in the process of swinging into action.

I hadn't seen Siobhan until late that night, after I'd been extracted from the clutches of the LAPD, who'd been arguing jurisdiction with the FBI when Ben and a bunch of lawyers had turned up with a court order to snatch me away.

"Of course Hydesmith had a phone," Siobhan had said when we were reunited. "It was so tiny and had so many functions it took me a minute to work out how to use it. Then I called your Ben — nice guy, by the way — and set everything in motion."

Now the whole lot of them were being held in Federal prison, awaiting trial. Tecla and Jason, it was rumored, were considering a plea bargain that would spare their lives in return for copious information on SHO's activities and Edward Hydesmith's active role in the bioterrorism plot. Edward Hydesmith, for his part, was relying on a platoon of the highest profile, and most expensive lawyers in America. Gail and Innis were both singing loudly. The members of Red Wolf's team were being held incommunicado while their real identities were established. Various smaller fish, including Carmina, and been swept up in the net and were cooperating with the authorities.

"You know," said Siobhan, rolling over to rub suntan oil

167

on my back, "you're not really appreciated in ASIO. You've seen what a wonderful team we make together."

"True," I said.

"So how about it? I'd love you to join the Hurdstone Foundation. And my father's all for it."

I smiled into her eyes. "Maybe," I said. "Maybe I will . . ."

ABOUT THE AUTHOR

CLAIRE McNAB is the author of fourteen Detective Inspector Carol Ashton mysteries: *Lessons in Murder, Fatal Reunion, Death Down Under, Cop Out, Dead Certain, Body Guard, Double Bluff, Inner Circle, Chain Letter, Past Due, Set Up, Under Suspicion, Death Club,* and *Accidental Murder.* She has written two romances, *Under the Southern Cross* and *Silent Heart,* and has co-authored a self-help book, *The Loving Lesbian,* with Sharon Gedan. She is the author of four Denise Cleever thrillers, *Murder Undercover, Death Understood, Out of Sight,* and *Recognition Factor.*

In her native Australia, Claire is known for her crime fiction, plays, children's novels, and self-help books.

Now permanently residing in Los Angeles, she teaches fiction writing in the UCLA Extension Writers' Program. She makes it a point to return to Australia once a year to refresh her Aussie accent.

Publications from
BELLA BOOKS, INC.
the best in contemporary lesbian fiction

P.O. Box 201007   Ferndale, MI 48220
Phone: 800-729-4992
www.bellabooks.com

RECOGNITION FACTOR: 4th Detective Denise Cleever
Thriller by Claire McNab. 176 pp. Denise Cleever tracks a
notorious terrorist to America.   ISBN 1-931513-24-4 $12.95

NORA AND LIZ by Nancy Garden. 296 pp. Lesbian romance by
the author of *Annie On My Mind*.   ISBN 1931513-20-1 $12.95

MIDAS TOUCH by Frankie J. Jones. 208 pp. Sandra had
everything but love.   ISBN 1-931513-21-X $12.95

BEYOND ALL REASON by Peggy J. Herring. 240 pp. A romance
hotter than Texas.   ISBN 1-9513-25-2 $12.95

ACCIDENTAL MURDER: 14th Detective Inspector Carol
Ashton Mystery by Claire McNab. 208 pp.Carol Ashton
tracks an elusive killer.   ISBN 1-931513-16-3 $12.95

SEEDS OF FIRE:Tunnel of Light Trilogy, Book 2 by Karin
Kallmaker writing as Laura Adams. 274 pp. Intriguing
sequel to *Sleight of Hand*.   ISBN 1-931513-19-8 $12.95

DRIFTING AT THE BOTTOM OF THE WORLD by
Auden Bailey. 288 pp. Beautifully written first novel set
in Antarctica.   ISBN 1-931513-17-1 $12.95

STREET RULES: A Detective Franco Mystery by
Baxter Clare. 304 pp. Gritty, fast-paced mystery with
compelling Detective L.A. Franco   ISBN 1-931513-14-7 $12.95

CLOUDS OF WAR by Diana Rivers. 288 pp. Women
unite to defend Zelindar!   ISBN 1-931513-12-0 $12.95

OUTSIDE THE FLOCK by Jackie Calhoun. 220 pp.
Searching for love, Jo finds temptation. ISBN 1-931513-13-9 $12.95

WHEN GOOD GIRLS GO BAD: A Motor City Thriller by
Therese Szymanski. 230 pp. Brett, Randi, and Allie join
forces to stop a serial killer.   ISBN 1-931513-11-2 $12.95

DEATHS OF JOCASTA: 2nd Micky Night Mystery by J.M.
Redmann. 408 pp. Sexy and intriguing Lambda Literary Award
nominated mystery.   ISBN 1-931513-10-4 $12.95

LOVE IN THE BALANCE by Marianne K. Martin. 256 pp.
The classic lesbian love story, back in print!
                                         ISBN 1-931513-08-2 $12.95

THE COMFORT OF STRANGERS by Peggy J. Herring.
272 pp. Lela's work was her passion . . . until now.
ISBN 1-931513-09-0 $12.95

CHICKEN by Paula Martinac. 208 pp. Lynn finds that the
only thing harder than being in a lesbian relationship is
ending one.   ISBN 1-931513-07-4 $11.95

TAMARACK CREEK by Jackie Calhoun. 208 pp. An intriguing story of love and danger.   ISBN 1-931513-06-6 $11.95

DEATH BY THE RIVERSIDE: 1st Micky Knight Mystery by
J.M. Redmann. 320 pp. Finally back in print, the book that
launched the Lambda Literary Award winning Micky Knight
mystery series.   ISBN 1-931513-05-8 $11.95

EIGHTH DAY: A Cassidy James Mystery by Kate Calloway.
272 pp. In the eighth installment of the Cassidy James
mystery series, Cassidy goes undercover at a camp for
troubled teens.   ISBN 1-931513-04-X $11.95

MIRRORS by Marianne K. Martin. 208 pp. Jean Carson and
Shayna Bradley fight for a future together.
ISBN 1-931513-02-3 $11.95

THE ULTIMATE EXIT STRATEGY: A Virginia Kelly
Mystery by Nikki Baker. 240 pp. The long-awaited return of
the wickedly observant Virginia Kelly.   ISBN 1-931513-03-1 $11.95

FOREVER AND THE NIGHT by Laura DeHart Young.
224 pp. Desire and passion ignite the frozen Arctic in this
exciting sequel to the classic romantic adventure *Love on
the Line*.   ISBN 0-931513-00-7 $11.95

WINGED ISIS by Jean Stewart. 240 pp. The long-awaited
sequel to *Warriors of Isis* and the fourth in the exciting
Isis series.   ISBN 1-931513-01-5 $11.95

ROOM FOR LOVE by Frankie J. Jones. 192 pp. Jo and
Beth must overcome the past in order to have a future
together.   ISBN 0-9677753-9-6 $11.95

THE QUESTION OF SABOTAGE by Bonnie J. Morris.
144 pp. A charming, sexy tale of romance, intrigue, and
coming of age.   ISBN 0-9677753-8-8 $11.95

SLEIGHT OF HAND by Karin Kallmaker writing as
Laura Adams. 256 pp. A journey of passion, heartbreak
and triumph that reunites two women for a final chance
at their destiny.   ISBN 0-9677753-7-X $11.95

MOVING TARGETS: A Helen Black Mystery by Pat Welch.
240 pp. Helen must decide if getting to the bottom of a
mystery is worth hitting bottom.   ISBN 0-9677753-6-1 $11.95

CALM BEFORE THE STORM by Peggy J. Herring. 208
pp. Colonel Robicheaux retires from the military and
comes out of the closet.   ISBN 0-9677753-1-0 $12.95

OFF SEASON by Jackie Calhoun. 208 pp. Pam threatens
Jenny and Rita's fledgling relationship. ISBN 0-9677753-0-2 $11.95

**Visit
Bella Books
at
www.bellabooks.com**